"What would really scare you?"

Blackie asked the question with unexpected solemnity, after his earlier playfulness.

Jenny shuddered a bit. "I once saw *Dr. Jekyll and Mr. Hyde*—the version with Spencer Tracy. There was something terrifying about the way he changed. I suppose the idea of two personalities in one body frightens me as much as anything."

"That's very interesting," Blackie murmured. But he sounded far away, absorbed in private thoughts. "More frightening than the movie we saw tonight?" he asked suddenly.

He slanted her a look that sent shivers of excitement down her spine. A look that told Jenny he was as attracted to her as she was to him.

"Most horror-movie villains are terrifying on the outside all the time," she said slowly. "But Mr. Hyde was lurking just beneath the surface and you never knew when he'd emerge. A lot of husbands are like that after marriage, Blackie."

"So are a lot of wives," he retorted.

Rebecca Winters, an American writer and mother of four, is a graduate of the University of Utah, who has also studied overseas at schools in Switzerland and France, including the Sorbonne. She is currently teaching French and Spanish to junior high school students. Despite her busy schedule, Rebecca always finds time to write. She's already researching the background for her next Harlequin Romance!

Books by Rebecca Winters

BLACKIE'S WOMAN
Rebecca Winters

Harlequin Books

TORONTO • NEW YORK • LONDON
AMSTERDAM • PARIS • SYDNEY • HAMBURG
STOCKHOLM • ATHENS • TOKYO • MILAN

ISBN 0-373-03144-0

Harlequin Romance first edition August 1991

BLACKIE'S WOMAN

CHAPTER ONE

JENNIFER O'BRIEN left her trailer with five minutes to spare before she was due to report for work. As day manager of the O'Brien's Restaurant across the highway, she was required to be on the job promptly at seven. But a familiar sense of grief and desolation swept over her as she climbed into the air-conditioned cab of her dad's Chevy pickup, and she simply sat there, without starting the engine.

Through the heat waves dancing off the desert floor, she could see in the distance the odd conglomeration of gasoline pumps, museum and restaurant that had been her refuge for the past month. Had she really been on the job only thirty days? It felt more like ten years.

She'd never worked so hard in her life. Each day presented a whole new set of problems. More and more she felt unequal to the task, and her doubts robbed her of any modicum of confidence she did possess. That was fast disappearing anyway, because the pampered shallow existence she'd led until recently had in no way prepared her to come to the desert to do real work.

Under the circumstances, she was surprised that her boss, Tom Burch, hadn't said something about her far-from-perfect performance before now, though he had no inkling of her true identity. Had he known who she really was, Jenny felt sure he'd never have hired her. She'd discovered that her reputation as the rich, spoiled and irresponsible Jennifer O'Brien preceded her wherever she went. So she'd used her mother's maiden name, Connelly, when applying for the management-trainee position. But guilt at deceiving Tom was weighing her down. Soon she'd have to tell him the truth.

Those ever-present tears filled her eyes as she stared at the restaurant. It was Donald O'Brien's legacy, a standing testimonial to the transplanted Irishman who turned a simple hot-dog stand into a multimillion-dollar family restaurant chain renowned throughout California and several adjoining states.

To Jenny, the restaurant was a reminder that her father was dead. She still had trouble believing he hadn't survived his unexpected heart attack. What made it even more nightmarish was the unpalatable fact that she'd been out of the country on a partying junket when he'd been stricken. The man she'd adored had died without her being there to hold his hand or to tell him how much she loved him.

Regret over so many things left unsaid deepened Jenny's sorrow. Now she could never ask his forgiveness for her impossible behavior, could never explain what had motivated it. She'd never be able to thank him for using his money and clout to bail her out of the numerous scrapes that had made her a favorite target for the press.

Donald O'Brien's grief over his wife's early death had driven him to focus all his energies on the business. His obsession with work made Jenny feel excluded, and in her pain, she became a rebellious teenager, albeit a rich one. Starved for her father's attention, she was willing to go to any lengths to get it because she worshiped him and needed the fatherly companionship he seemed incapable of giving her.

Yet like most young people, she thought her dynamic father would live forever. It never occurred to her, even as an adult, that there wouldn't be plenty of time to grow closer as father and daughter. Time to discuss the future of the company and his expressed wish that she learn the business and take over the helm once he retired. But he'd died before that could happen....

After two months, she still couldn't believe he was gone. She had no brothers or sisters with whom to share her grief and had never felt more alone in her life. The crowd she'd been running around with for the past year couldn't really be called friends. Not one of them had phoned or tried to see her since her father's death. And most of her old college friends had married and moved away.

Donald O'Brien's death had left Jenny a wealthy woman, *an heiress*. She'd grown to hate the term because, particularly since the funeral, money seemed to be the only thing on people's minds.

She'd been besieged with advice from her father's attorneys and the company's board of directors, urging her to sell the controlling interest she'd inherited. Couching their arguments in the nicest possible way, of course, they pointed out that she didn't know the food industry, and couldn't contribute anything significant as a member of the board.

But behind her back, everyone associated with O'Brien's knew her as Donny's irresponsible, headstrong daughter who'd been unavailable when her father died. She'd made a mockery of her life up to now and the board of directors knew it.

Jenny couldn't help feeling swayed by their arguments; she was too overcome by sorrow and guilt to think clearly. At the time of her father's fatal heart attack she'd been dancing the night away on a Greek shipping magnate's yacht.

When word of her father's illness finally reached her through Vi Allen, his private secretary, Donald O'Brien was already dead. For the first time in twenty-five years Jenny's absorption in her own pleasure, which masked the pain of her father's seeming indifference, had ended in a crisis that turned her world upside down. It was a sober grief-stricken Jennifer O'Brien who'd flown home to bury her father.

She'd never seriously entertained the idea of taking over his business—the business that had kept them apart. And judging by the reaction of the board, everyone else found it equally absurd.

The only person telling her *not* to sell was Vi. And it was Vi who challenged Jenny to do some soul-searching and prove she could make a success of her life. Now was the time to show the world that she'd inherited her father's business sense; now was the time to show that she valued his achievements. Not only had he been crazy about his "darlin' Jenny," Vi told her, it'd been his lifelong wish that she fill his shoes. Why not spend a year finding out what she was really made of—and try to prove him right? And in the process, reverse people's negative opinions?

As the older woman continued to plead her case, Jenny's eyes were opened to another truth. *Vi had loved her father!* When Jenny probed a little deeper, Vi admitted she would've married him if he'd asked her, but he never did and both she and Jenny knew why. Donald O'Brien had mourned his wife until the day he died.

The frank talk with Vi, who'd understood the real reasons for the years of frivolous behavior, was like a healing balm to Jenny's soul. She felt a new closeness to the loyal supportive woman who confessed she'd always love Jenny and would've liked her for a daughter. Humbled by Vi's admission, Jenny felt compelled to listen to the older woman's advice.

"Tom Burch is your dad's best manager in the chain. He'll teach you everything you need to know about the restaurant business. No one on the board knew anything about running a company before they'd worked their way up the ranks. Why not learn from Tom what goes on at O'Brien's before making a decision you might regret for the rest of your life?"

At this point Vi's opinion carried a great deal of weight with Jenny. Not only that, what she said made perfect sense. Though Donald O'Brien might not have expressed his feelings, Vi convinced Jenny that her father loved her more than she could imagine. That assurance had ultimately brought Jenny to the desert. She could think of no better way to honor her father than to try to carry on his life's work. But she was terrified of failing.

Vi had written a glowing reference describing Jenny's capabilities, referring to her college degree—in reality undistinguished—and her work experience. As a lark, Jenny had occasionally waited tables at the O'Brien's close to home in Santa Barbara during high school. But it was on a show-up-when-you-want, leave-when-you-want basis.

Vi stretched the truth by presenting Jenny as a dedicated worker, someone with the potential to rise in the company. Fortunately for Jenny, Tom hadn't come to her father's funeral because of his asthma problems, so he had no idea who she really was. That, plus Vi's creative wording, must have helped Jenny make it to the final interview. But as Vi pointed out, it was Jenny herself who impressed Tom enough to land the job.

On a sigh of determination, Jenny started the engine and drove the short distance to the restaurant. She'd need the truck later to drive into Baker for some supplies that hadn't arrived on the Trailways bus.

She stepped out of the cab into the full fury of a scorching July day. Even this early in the morning, the heat was almost unbearable. Before she wilted on the spot, she quickly made her way to the restaurant through the parking area, filled with tankers and semis.

The icy cold interior was heavenly. While Jenny stood beneath the blower to cool down, Betty, the cashier, approached her. "There's a man in your office looking for a job. He's been waiting an hour or more. Just thought you'd like to know."

Jenny glanced at her watch. It was exactly seven o'clock. "Why didn't you send him in to Tom? He does the interviewing."

Betty shook her head. "Not anymore. Tom says you're in charge of everything now, and that includes personnel." Her eyebrows lifted expressively as she gave Jenny a friendly smile and went back to her post.

A light film of perspiration broke out on Jenny's brow. On the one hand she was pleased and surprised that Tom had enough confidence in her to entrust her with the hiring and firing of employees. But she'd never conducted an interview before. In fact, her only experience with that sort of thing had been her own interview with Tom, when *she'd* been the one applying for the job.

As she hurried to the office, she tried to remember how Tom had gone about it. Deep in thought, she didn't realize the office door was being pushed open until it was too late. A dark-haired man strode out and Jenny stumbled in an effort to avoid bumping into him. His hands shot out to support her. For a moment she was held tightly against a solid male chest.

She gasped softly, not only from the unexpected contact but because of the iridescent blue eyes ranging over her face.

"Are you all right?" the man asked in a deep voice that sounded as if it came from somewhere on the East Coast. In that instant, she had the distinct impression she'd seen him somewhere before. Perhaps in Europe?

"Yes, of course," she said, nodding. She felt more than a little disturbed by the sensation of his lean powerful body so close to hers, by the warmth of his hands on her upper arms. "I'm afraid I had something on my mind and didn't look where I was going. Are you the gentleman here about a job?"

The man still holding her seemed fascinated by her cloudy gray eyes gazing up at him through velvety black lashes. "That's right," he murmured, slowly relinquishing his hold. "You're the manager?" His eyes flared with interest.

Jenny swallowed hard. "Yes. I'm Ms. Connelly, and I'm afraid there are no openings at the moment, but you're welcome to fill out an application in case a position comes available."

A palpable tension hovered between them. "Do you always make snap decisions? Have you stopped to consider that I might be exactly the person you've always looked for, but never found?" He made no move to step away. His self-confidence bordered on arrogance, Jenny thought incredulously.

"If you were president of the United States, I still couldn't offer you a job that doesn't exist!" she retorted.

She regretted her words the minute they were out, knowing she'd just failed her first test in the personnel department. Flippant remarks meant as put-downs belonged in the past and had no place in her new life.

Hadn't Tom taught her the customer is always right? A good manager could handle any situation and come out on top, provided he or she remained cool and levelheaded, and retained a healthy sense of humor.

Furious at making such a blunder, Jenny backed away to put distance between them and noted the glimmer of amusement in his shrewd regard. It gave her the impetus to pull herself together.

With a nonchalance she was far from feeling, she said, "You make a good case for yourself, Mr...."

"Archer. Blackie Archer." His lips twitched provocatively, as if her quick recovery pleased him. Jenny shivered. How was she going to make it through a whole interview with him? The opening lines from one of her favorite L. E. Boyd mysteries came to mind. "Rita was the best cop on the beat. Intrepid, gutsy. Danger was only a game until Mulvaney showed up and redefined the word for all time."

Now that they were several inches apart, she noted his well-worn jeans and pale blue work shirt with the sleeves rolled up to the elbows.

His physique qualified him to drive one of those huge gasoline tankers she'd seen parked outside by the pumps. Maybe he'd stopped here on cross-country hauls and liked the atmosphere. But she quickly dismissed the idea of his being a trucker when she noticed that his forearms were the same color as the skin on his face and neck.

Unlike most Californians, he didn't have a tan and his complexion seemed almost pale, making his hair look more black than dark brown in comparison. The lines around his blue eyes and sensual mouth led her to believe he was in his early thirties. He intimidated with a glance. Jenny suspected that this was a man who never backed down, no matter what.

She felt an unwilling attraction to his classic good looks and the slow tantalizing smile that lifted one corner of his mouth. Jenny had traveled many places and met a lot of men, but she'd never encountered anyone she found more exciting than this stranger. Still, she couldn't dismiss the feeling she'd seen him somewhere before.

His penetrating gaze shouldn't have disturbed her so much. She was used to attention from men, used to their frank stares of admiration. But this man's perusal went far beyond that.

She wore a tailored sleeveless cotton shirtwaist dress in pale pink. It was modest and comfortable, yet she felt vulnerable as his eyes wandered over her full curves and long legs. By the time he'd finished his appraisal, she knew her face was as flaming as the red-gold hair cascading to her shoulders. She had the strangest feeling he could hear her heart pounding and divine the errant thoughts running through her mind.

She cleared her throat. "I understand you've been waiting an hour or more, but I didn't come on duty until now. Please. Sit down." She motioned for him to follow her back inside the small office, which contained a desk, file cabinet and half a dozen chairs. The room was used for a variety of functions and served as the management-trainee office.

He lounged in one of the chairs opposite her desk, looking almost insolently at ease.

"I'd prefer if you'd fill out the application first, then we'll talk," she said, trying to sound brisk and businesslike.

"That makes sense."

Unnerved by his vaguely mocking air, Jenny turned her back on him while she hunted down the appropriate form. She prayed her nervousness didn't show as she opened the top drawer, still not well acquainted with the filing system set up by Tom's wife, Marva.

To her relief, she found the file under the *A*s and pulled the two-paged form from the folder. She fastened it to a clipboard, rummaged for a pen in the drawer and handed them to him.

"Be as thorough as you can, considering you *might* just be the man I've been looking for but never found."

He lifted one eyebrow. "Since the feeling's entirely mutual, Ms. Connelly, I'll make a point of being as thorough as possible."

Too late she realized her mistake and felt her cheeks flush with embarrassment. She sounded like a tease instead of a poised mature businesswoman who was in charge of the situation.

"Take as long as you need."

He rubbed the back of his neck and stared at her thoughtfully. "How much do you want to know?"

She sensed that he wasn't talking about the job and her face grew hotter. Too uncomfortable to remain in the same room with him, she used the excuse that she was needed in the kitchen and made her escape. But even after she'd closed the door, she thought she could feel his scrutiny.

For the next half hour she kept herself busy checking the waitress stations, making sure they were clean and amply stocked. But every minute of that time, her mind was on Blackie Archer. With those lean dark good looks, he was easily the most attractive male she'd ever met. And the most aggressive...

"I was afraid you'd forgotten about me and I had half a mind to come looking for you," he quipped when she finally went back to her office.

Little did he know how close she'd come to asking Tom to conduct the interview. But that would have been admitting defeat. Tom would assume she didn't have what it took to be an O'Brien's manager. At this stage, she didn't want to risk his disappointment in her. Jenny had already committed herself to becoming the kind of manager her father would have been proud of.

"Some people take longer than others to fill everything out," she explained with feigned calm, once again sitting down at her desk. "It's been my experience that most applicants are more at ease if they're given some privacy." He couldn't know she was speaking of her one and only experience.

"On that point I tend to agree." He rose from the chair and leaned forward to hand her the application, making her keenly aware of his closeness and the pleasant aroma of his musky after-shave.

She scanned the contents. Thirty-two years old, a college graduate, single, never been arrested, well-traveled. Home address New York City, currently staying at the same trailer park as she was. Last two jobs: temporary assistant cook on a schooner sailing the Caribbean, temporary physical-therapy aide in a North Carolina hospital. He'd listed their phone numbers.

Her first thought was that she couldn't have met him before because he wasn't the kind of man a woman could forget. He still looked familiar, though.

Her next thought was that, with his education, why had he been doing the kinds of jobs he'd listed? Her last thought was that he couldn't possibly be serious about a job at O'Brien's. What kind of game was he playing?

Trying to avoid any more blunders, Jenny took her time before responding. "I notice you've requested only temporary work. It seems to be the only kind of work you do."

"That's right. I understand your restaurant is open twenty-four hours a day, 365 days a year. Perhaps you're in need of custodial or maintenance assistance."

She took a deep breath. "Don't you think you'd get bored here, considering you have an economics degree from one of the most prestigious Eastern universities?" She tried not to sound too judgmental.

He pinned her with a level look. "After a few years, economics began to bore me and I turned to other pursuits. I quite enjoy my life-style, which teaches me a variety of new skills, yet allows me the freedom to explore untried territory."

Jenny tapped a pencil against her cheek, endeavoring to handle this as Tom would. "When you say temporary, how long are you talking about?"

He folded his arms across his broad chest. "Anywhere from six weeks to three months."

"And money is no object?" In the box marked "expected salary," he'd put the minimum wage.

His sudden white smile dazzled her. "No. It's the job itself that interests me." The caress of his eyes couldn't have been more obvious. Again Jenny was forced to keep her thoughts to herself. A lot more than the job interested Blackie Archer, but she had to let it go for the moment if she wanted to stay in control.

She eyed him covertly. He was too polished, too sophisticated and urbane to be applying for a job usually filled by students or retired people. He had to have an undisclosed source of income!

Something wasn't right. If Tom were here right now, she was positive he'd agree with her. She moistened her lips and to her consternation the stranger registered the betraying gesture.

Sitting back in the swivel chair, she tried to assume an air of dignity, but he wasn't fooled. "I have to admit that out here in the desert, good custodial help is hard to come by. I'd seriously consider you for a number of jobs, *if* there was an opening. But there isn't. I'm very sorry, Mr. Archer. Still, I'll keep your application on file, and if an appropriate position does present itself, I'll notify you."

He made no move to leave. "Since there can't be that many people with good references anxious to work in such isolated circumstances, why don't you create a job for me? Even if it's only for a few hours a day—or night, as the case may be. I simply want the opportunity to work here. I'll do any task. You won't be sorry." To his credit, he sounded completely earnest. But this early in her career, Jenny didn't dare take on that kind of responsibility.

"I wish I could do that, Mr. Archer. In any event, I have to check out your references. If everything's in order, you'll be notified as soon as a job turns up."

Frowning, he rose to his full height. "I'll warn you now. I'm not taking your decision as final. I'll be back, Ms. Connelly." On that warning, he strode out of her office, his bearing no less assured than before.

After he'd gone Jenny rested her elbows on the desk and rubbed her aching temples with her fingertips. The man was an enigma. If he did come back she'd ask Tom to handle him, but in fact she doubted Blackie Archer would return and wondered why the thought gave her this curious sense of loss. It didn't make sense.

On impulse she decided to phone the two employers listed on his application, if only to satisfy her curiosity about the man and establish his veracity. To her astonishment, both jobs turned out to be legitimate and Blackie received glowing accolades for his work. He was welcome back at either job any time in the future.

There was one thing she could say for him: his references were flawless. But she still had questions about his real motives for wanting to work at O'Brien's.

Thoughts of Blackie Archer and their strange interview filled her mind as she drove into Baker to pick up the load of new glasses and mugs that hadn't, for some reason, been sent on the bus. While she was there she did some personal shopping and mailed a letter to Vi.

On her return, she asked a couple of busboys to unload the truck while she grabbed a bite of lunch in the dining room. The rest of the afternoon would be devoted to paperwork. Tom insisted she should familiarize herself with the books, and she realized he was right. Until she understood the accounting system, standardized for all the restaurants, she wouldn't have a grasp of O'Brien's inner workings.

While she drank her root beer and waited for one of the waitresses to bring her a sandwich, her eyes wandered around the room. There were a hundred O'Brien's Restaurants in California, Nevada and Arizona, every one of them identical. The interior was meant to resemble an eighteenth-century Irish country inn, with dark wooden beams, floors and tables. She thought of her father and his business genius as she admired the green-and-white curtains fastened at the leaded windows.

The same color scheme was carried out in the wait-resses' shamrock-green skirts, white peasant blouses and black waistcoats laced up the front. Her father didn't like to see women in pants and deplored fashions that dressed women like men.

As a result, Jenny had grown up with two wardrobes. One to please her father when he was home, the other full of designer jeans and tops to please herself. Now he wasn't there to notice what she wore. The thought brought more pain and she tried to concentrate on matters at hand.

Strangely drained by her encounter with Blackie Archer, she didn't relish the prospect of going back to her office to study ledgers for the rest of the day. But it was just as well she did have work to do. It might keep her from thinking about him. Besides, the air-conditioning in the restaurant was ten times more efficient than the unit in her trailer.

O'Brien's spared no expense in keeping things cold. No wonder truck drivers and tourists stopped here. It was a delightfully cool semidark oasis away from the blistering summer sun that caused the temperature to soar to 115 degrees in the shade most days.

The clock said two-thirty, a little late for lunch, yet every table was full. This particular restaurant was open year-round. Vi had compiled a file on it for her; according to statistics, this O'Brien's—located in the Mojave desert, miles from the nearest town, Barstow—had the most repeat business and steadily growing profits of any restaurant in the chain.

Looking around at the bustling conviviality of patrons and employees alike, Jenny had to remind herself of the no man's land that lay outside the door.

Her meal arrived as she drained the last of her drink. Famished because she'd skipped breakfast, she began eating her tuna-salad sandwich, only to lose her appetite when she noticed a tall dark-haired man enter the dining room. Her heart immediately gave a funny kick.

His eyes scanned the room until his gaze locked with hers, then he walked purposefully toward her, drawing the attention of several interested female tourists. Jenny's pulse started to race, and she put the remainder of her sandwich back on the plate.

"Do you mind if I join you?" he asked without preamble. His question was rhetorical since he sat down opposite her and made himself at home, unwrapping a package of crackers from the basket. She watched his strong even teeth as he bit into the first one.

"Be my guest," she murmured dryly, wishing his masculine appeal wasn't quite so potent. One corner of his mouth lifted in a devastating smile meant to charm a female down to her toenails.

"Have you had time to come to any conclusions about hiring me? If you take the trouble to check my references, you'll discover they're impeccable." In a surprising gesture, he reached out to remove a dab of mayonnaise from the corner of her mouth. "I couldn't resist," he said softly.

The intimacy angered her, not only because of his effrontery, but because his touch shouldn't have shot through her body like a bolt of electricity.

"If you want a job so badly, you're going about it entirely the wrong way. As I told you this morning, there are no openings, Mr. Archer. Now if you don't mind, I'd like to finish my lunch.''

"Of course I don't mind," he said, his voice infuriatingly calm. "And while you eat, I'll be more than happy to fill you in on any details about myself that weren't required on the application. Perhaps by the end of your meal, you'll have changed your mind about easing me into O'Brien's work force.''

The familiar surge of adrenaline let Jenny know this had gone far enough. Here was a problem that called for Tom's expertise. She pushed back her chair and started to get up. Blackie forestalled her movement by reaching across the table and covering her hand in a firm grip, which forced her to remain seated.

Her startled gaze flew to his. The determination in those steady blue eyes unnerved Jenny. Her head reared back, and her coppery mane of hair flounced around her shoulders.

"You're going to be extremely sorry if you don't let go of me," she warned in her lowest, iciest voice, not wishing to make a scene in front of dozens of innocent diners. In the past, that frosty tone had cut more than one presumptuous male to shreds.

"My father," she was about to say, but caught herself, suddenly remembering that he was no longer alive. This time he couldn't extricate her from one of her precarious situations. But at least she could honestly say she'd done nothing to bring on this particular problem.

"I want five minutes of your time, Ms. Connelly. That's all. If you still want to call the police when I'm through talking, I won't stop you.''

CHAPTER TWO

HIS LAST REMARK denied her the satisfaction of delivering her final withering ultimatum. It galled her that he could read her mind with such ease.

"What's it going to be?" he taunted. "I can continue to hold your hand, which I assure you is no penance at all. People will assume we're lovers. Or I can let it go. But only on the understanding that you'll stay seated until I explain why I need a job in your particular restaurant."

He'd placed her in an impossible position and she resented it, but she made her decision.

"You have five minutes, Mr. Archer, but after that you're on your own. I hope I've made myself clear." The light of battle glittered in her stormy gray eyes.

"Perfectly." His disarming grin knocked the foundation out from under her. When he freed her hand, she remained rigidly in place, her nerves coiled like springs. It seemed incredible that people at the surrounding tables were eating and enjoying pleasant conversation, unaware that this...this throwback to a buccaneer had blackmailed her into listening to him.

"Your time is running out," she hissed.

A mysterious smile broke out on his face as he reached into his back pocket for his wallet. "I was hoping I could talk you into hiring me without having to bare my soul. But you're too good at your job, Ms. Connelly. You obviously need a lot more convincing since you're not going to take me on my charms alone."

Steeling herself not to be mollified by those very charms, she watched through narrowed eyes as he pulled out some identification and flashed it in front of her. The card was stamped OFFICIAL PRESS. But it was CORBIN BLACKWELL, JOURNALIST that leapt out at her. The black-and-white photo didn't do justice to the vital living presence of one of the nation's most famous and celebrated journalists.

No wonder he looked familiar! Jenny's father, a voracious reader and philosopher of no small mind, had read Corbin Blackwell's syndicated column every week of his life—*before* he devoured the business sections of the *Los Angeles Times, Chicago Tribune, New York Times, Wall Street Journal* and half a dozen other major newspapers from overseas!

When Jenny finally lifted her gaze, she surprised a disarming look of entreaty in his. "I take it you know who I am. And you're wondering what in hell I'm doing here making your life miserable, so I'll tell you the truth. I need background on the lives of waitresses and truckers for a series of articles I'm working on.

"The information in question isn't something I can glean from secondary sources—books or other articles. I need hands-on experience, to observe from the inside, so to speak. I've interviewed dozens of cross-country truckers already, even driven a semi for a stretch to get the feel, and 'O'Brien's in the Mojave' has been the one restaurant repeatedly brought up in conversations. You have a reputation for the best food and the best service of just about any place, coast to coast.''

Jenny averted her head, stunned by his revelations. Her father would have loved to hear this kind of praise, especially from the renowned Corbin Blackwell.

''Do you always go by the name of Blackie Archer when you're in search of a story?''

''That's right. Archer's my mother's maiden name. I have to keep a low profile. Otherwise, the minute people know who I am, they step out of character and I've lost that intrinsic element I'm looking for. They start to perform roles—giving me what they think I want instead of being themselves. I was hoping you'd hire me on for a temporary period doing anything you could drum up. I wouldn't ask for a salary, but it might look odd if I came to work and didn't get a paycheck like everyone else.

''My other alternative is to hang around for the next six weeks or so, but playing tourist wouldn't take me behind the scenes to observe the inner workings and get a real sense of the personalities. And that's what I'm after. So I'm placing myself at your mercy, Ms. Connelly.''

He darted a glance at his watch. ''My five minutes are up.'' He didn't say ''You can call the police now,'' because he knew she wouldn't. ''Am I forgiven for my unorthodox way of handling this job interview? You have every right to throw me out on my ear, you know. In fact, I'm growing more and more intrigued, wondering why I'm still sitting here, enjoying myself more than I ever thought possible.''

She managed a weak smile. "Mr. Blackwell, I'm sure you understand why I reacted with some...hesitation."

He answered her smile with a lopsided one of his own. "I take it I won't be carted off to jail. I'm relieved. I've spent more nights there than I'd care to remember."

"Does that mean you lied on the application form? I thought you'd never been arrested."

"I haven't. But in order to do a series of articles on prison life, I went behind bars for a time. It was one of my more sobering experiences to date. Worse in some ways than war zones I've covered."

"Isn't the research about truckers and waitresses a rather abrupt departure from your normal pursuits?" she couldn't help asking. "Don't you usually work on bigger stories?"

He waved to one of the waitresses and asked for coffee, then gave Jenny his full attention. "It's not really a departure, no," he said thoughtfully. "Journalists are always looking for the story that brings a human dimension to circumstances or events. The so-called human-interest story, wherever or whatever it might be. Sometimes the most compelling stories are the ones played out on the home front. Truckers and waitresses form a big part of the backbone of our country." He eyed her over the rim of his cup. "Without them, you and I wouldn't be here sharing a meal."

Jenny blinked. How many times had she heard her father express those exact sentiments, those same beliefs about the importance of a waitress's work? In fact, Donald O'Brien had established a scholarship fund for the best employees in his company, not only as an incentive but as a way of honoring them.

"Do I detect a ray of hope?" Corbin Blackwell asked huskily.

Jenny couldn't sustain his stare, and she took a drink of water to avoid giving him an immediate answer. "I—I can't make any promises at this stage, but there's a dishwasher working day shift who's asked to be promoted. It's possible you could take over his job until I can find a permanent replacement, but I'll have to do some checking first."

How was she going to tell Tom she'd hired the first person she'd ever interviewed, for an opening that didn't yet exist?

"I take it you're referring to my references?" His mouth twitched sensually, making her pulses come alive.

"This conversation would never have taken place if I hadn't already spoken to your former employers concerning your excellent work record, Mr. Blackwell."

"Blackie," he corrected warmly. "And it means you were interested enough to follow up on my application—before you knew my real identity." Unexpectedly he got to his feet. "You've made my day, Ms. Connelly, whatever you decide." He put a five-dollar bill on the table. "When can I expect an answer—one way or the other?"

Not wanting to feel at any more of a disadvantage, she stood up, too, her sandwich only half-eaten. "I'll look into the matter right away. Where can you be reached?"

"I'm staying in one of those trailers across the highway."

The fact that he was already installed at the trailer court meant there'd been no question in his mind that he'd be hired. But she supposed someone didn't become a famous journalist without possessing an extraordinary amount of confidence.

"I'll leave word at the trailer office."

He studied her face, lingering on the soft curve of her mouth. "I'll be waiting."

"TOM? YOU BUSY?"

"I'm never too busy for you. Come on in, Jenny, and tell me what you've been up to." Jenny was officially off duty at six, and she'd come directly to Tom's office, anxious to make a clean breast of her dealings with Blackie. If she'd done the wrong thing, it was better to know now so she could still withdraw her tentative offer to Blackwell before too much damage had been done.

Tom, who was just finishing a call with the home office in Santa Barbara, waved her into a chair opposite his desk. He was short and slight with a thatch of wheat-colored hair. His square face was wreathed in a permanent smile that transformed his unremarkable features and hazel eyes.

For the hundredth time, Jenny wished she'd taken an interest in her father's business; if she had, she would have become friends with Tom, his oldest and most trusted manager, long before now. Deceiving Tom was causing her more than one restless night. She doubted she could last another couple of weeks without telling him the truth—that she was Donald O'Brien's infamous daughter.

Tom winked at her as he tried to end the phone conversation, eliciting a smile from Jenny who looked around his office with its dozens of awards and manager-of-the-year plaques.

There were photos, as well, and she focused her attention on several that showed her father standing next to Tom as they grinned into the camera. Some of the shots had to be twenty years old or more. Despite herself, tears formed every time she studied her father's smiling face.

"Okay. What's giving you headaches?" he asked at last, perching himself on the corner of his desk. "Accounts receivable or debits?"

"Neither. At least, not yet." She wiped away traces of tears with her fingers. He could see she was disturbed, but he had the courtesy not to probe. "I've tentatively hired a new dishwasher, pending your approval of course."

He leaned forward, his hands on his knees. "And that's the problem causing you such distress?" Tom acted more like a father than an employer. In the short time she'd been in the desert, she'd grown attached to him and his wife. They were hardworking, easygoing and, above all, kind. An unbeatable combination, in Jenny's opinion.

"You might not approve of what I've done after you hear the details," she admitted, then rushed on with a full explanation. When she'd finished, she held her breath.

Tom remained poker-faced. "Do you want to know something, kiddo?"

"I—I'm not sure," Jenny muttered.

He scratched his head. "If you hadn't hired him, I'd have wondered what was wrong with you!"

Jenny jumped to her feet. "You mean that?"

"Don't I always mean what I say?" He grabbed her by the shoulders and hugged her. "We haven't had anything this exciting happen around here since Howard Hughes once stopped for lunch and left a one-thousand-dollar bill for a tip."

"You're kidding!" Jenny laughed, so relieved she'd done the right thing she was giddy.

"Nope." He shook his head. "It's the absolute truth. Now, as I see it, our biggest problem is going to be calling him Blackie and keeping a straight face. Can I tell Marva?"

Jenny rolled her eyes. "Don't you always tell Marva everything?"

He winked conspiratorially. "I sure do. And it's kept me out of a lot of trouble."

His comment, so innocently expressed, reminded Jenny once again that she hadn't been honest with Tom. On a more sober note, she said, "Thank you for your confidence in me. It means a great deal."

He paused before speaking. "You're coming along fine, Jenny. And just between you and me, I'd have hired him on the spot. Just about everybody who's anybody in these parts has walked through our doors at one time or other, but Corbin Blackwell is a celebrity of a different kind. For him to have picked us for research out of every other restaurant in the country is downright amazing. It's a darn shame Donny isn't around to hear about this!"

Jenny made a pretense of straightening her dress. Tom's affection for her father was evident in the nickname he used. Only a few close friends had called him Donny. "The credit goes to you, Tom, for running the kind of place truckers flock to. He'd have never picked us otherwise."

His face beamed. "You know what? You're as full of blarney as the head man himself used to be. For your information, a good manager needs to be something of a risk-taker. You have what it takes, kiddo. However, you're going to have to pay the price of that decision by teaching our star journalist how to wash dishes."

Tom chuckled as Jenny's eyes widened in surprise. "If Arlene's going to be training Ron, that leaves you to do the honors for Blackie. Think you can handle that and the books at the same time?"

Tom had just brought up something she hadn't even considered, which showed how inexperienced she really was. "I can handle it," she said with more confidence than she felt. The mere idea of teaching Corbin Blackwell anything, let alone how to wash dishes, gave her a fluttery feeling in the pit of her stomach.

"Good girl. Part of a manager's job is dealing with the unexpected. Anyway, this will be a good lesson for you—juggling several types of tasks at once. Say, when you talk to Blackie, tell him Marva and I'll be expecting him to join us for dinner in the private dining room tomorrow night. You're included in that, of course. Do you realize the places that man's been, the people he's interviewed?"

It did stagger the imagination and no one was more impressed than Jenny. "I'll relay the invitation. Thanks again, Tom."

The events of the day had pretty well drained Jenny. She couldn't wait to deliver her message and get back to her trailer for a shower and a meal.

The temperature gauge registered 112 as she left the restaurant and climbed into the seat of the pickup. She picked up the towel she kept in the truck so she could maneuver the steering wheel without burning her hands.

People were still pouring into the small museum next door as she started the engine. The sign advertised rattlesnakes as the main attraction; five dollars for adults, fifty cents for children. For a homemade sideshow, it brought in an amazing amount of money; it was Tom's own business, one he'd started as a small sideline years before. She couldn't help but wonder what Blackie would think of it.

Planning what she'd say to him in her note, she pulled away from the parking area and collided with a huge semi turning into a lay-by. The truck driver's expertise prevented a real disaster; the corner of her front fender was dented, but as far as she could tell, there'd been no damage to his truck.

She listened meekly as the driver gave her a fatherly lecture about paying more attention. This incident recalled others in the past when she hadn't been so lucky and had done thousands of dollars worth of damage to various expensive cars without counting the cost.

Damaging her father's favorite pickup, however, came as a real blow because she'd been trying so hard to do things right. Furious with herself for not concentrating, Jenny continued down the highway to the court, which housed thirty white trailers. Some were for tourists, others for the convenience of the restaurant's employees.

Feeling distinctly ill, she passed the trailer office without stopping. Delayed reaction had set in from the accident, and she was shaking when she reached the parking space next to her trailer. She doubted she could even get out of the cab. Her note to Blackie would have to wait.

It was then she heard the sound of a motorcycle pulling up beside her. She turned her head and for the third time that day she found herself gazing into those intense blue eyes.

"I saw what happened back there and I figured the heat must have got to you," he said with quiet amusement.

It was humiliating to realize he'd witnessed her latest disaster, but right now Jenny was too jittery to take offense. In fact, she felt slightly sick. What on earth was wrong with her?

"Are you all right?" he demanded, suddenly serious.

"Yes. I just need to sit here a minute."

He swung off his motorcycle with the grace of an athlete and covered the short distance between them in a few swift strides. "You're very pale—it's the shock. You need to get out of this heat," he said in a no-nonsense tone. "Give me your key so I can open your trailer."

Jenny handed it to him. In a matter of seconds, he'd dealt with the lock and returned to open the truck door.

"Out you come," he whispered, and lifted her easily from the cab. She'd gone limp from weakness and her head fell back over his arm. She closed her eyes as she felt her breathing grow shallow, all too aware of his closeness.

Jenny couldn't remember the last time a man had carried her in his arms, and she discovered that she enjoyed the sensation. Despite what people said about her, she'd never had a lover. In fact, she'd never been in love; lately she'd started to wonder if something was wrong with her because she'd never experienced more than mild interest in a man. She'd never lost even a shred of her cool composure—until today, with Blackie.

The trailer was blessedly cool. He managed to get both of them inside without bumping into anything, which said a great deal for his physical dexterity. After placing her on the flowered chintz spread of her bed, he studied her features, much as a doctor would examine his patient. This close she could make out the individual flecks of blue and silver in his incredible eyes.

His skin looked flushed, as if this was its first exposure to the sun in a long time. She felt the back of his hand against the softness of her hot cheek. "I bet you haven't eaten anything today, other than that sandwich. Which you didn't even finish."

"You're right, but I'm fine now."

"Wait there." His tone brooked no argument. He rummaged in her refrigerator, then pulled out a bottle of apple juice. When he'd poured a large glassful, he carried it over to her. She drank thirstily and felt somewhat revived.

"Thank you." She noticed the way he seemed to study the movement of her lips, which had probably lost any trace of lipstick. She, in turn, looked just as avidly at the laugh lines around his eyes and firm, shapely mouth.

"Little did I know the desire to hold you in my arms again would be fulfilled quite so soon," he murmured. Jenny closed her eyes, shutting out the intensity of his gaze. She prayed he wouldn't hear the wild thudding of her heart.

Heavens! If she didn't know he was trying to ingratiate himself to get a job, she'd probably have fallen for him without knowing what hit her. She'd met a lot of European men with charisma, but none of them had managed to stir up certain primitive female instincts the way this man did. She felt as if an unknown part of her, lying dormant, had suddenly leapt to life.

She had to put some distance between them. Getting up from the bed, she smoothed her hair and straightened her dress, trying to regain her equilibrium.

Blackie stood there, legs apart, hands resting on his hips—a totally male stance. "I was coming to find you for the express purpose of asking you to have dinner with me," he explained. "But under the circumstances, I'm going to bring dinner to you. I'll be right back."

He was gone before she could tell him not to bother, then, perversely, she decided there was no time to lose before he returned. After showering and getting dressed in white shorts and a sleeveless print blouse, she tidied the trailer and moved a pile of company printouts and memos from the table to make room for dinner.

She had no doubt that Blackie planned to eat with her. It might not be a bad idea. That way she could tell him they'd agreed to let him take the job. Explaining his duties ought to make for suitably impersonal conversation, she thought wryly. She could fill him in on the other staff, too. Tomorrow morning he'd be introduced as Blackie Archer, the dishwasher, and he'd receive exactly the same treatment as everyone else.

In no time at all she heard the sound of his motorcycle and soon he was knocking on the door. Still setting the table, she told him to come in.

"There's nothing I'd like to do more," he called back, "but this old man only has two hands and right now they're full of goodies."

Wiping the grin from her face, she walked to the door and opened it. He swept in, carrying what looked like enough food for a week. "You have style, Blackie," she said flippantly. "It won't be long before you're promoted from dishwasher to waiter."

"Is that your way of telling me I have a job?" he asked, eyeing her with disconcerting thoroughness as he put the food on the kitchen counter.

"That's right. You've been hired to wash dishes on the seven-to-four shift starting tomorrow morning. I can't tell you how long the job will last because I'm in the process of looking for a permanent dishwasher."

A light flared briefly in his eyes. "Thank you, Ms. Connelly. That sounds inadequate, considering you've done me a tremendous favor. I promise I won't let you down.''

"I'll hold you to that. You need to know I cleared this with my boss, Tom Burch. He's the general manager of O'Brien's. I had to tell him about you, but he and his wife will keep your identity a secret. They've invited you for dinner tomorrow night. Tom can hardly wait to meet you.''

A strange tension came between them. "Are you going to be there?''

"Yes.'' Suddenly shy, Jenny poked inside one of the sacks. "Thank you for dinner. Let's eat. Everything looks delicious.''

"Hamburgers are hamburgers.''

"But these are O'Brien hamburgers. Now that you're on the payroll, you're supposed to be aware of the difference.'' She emptied the sacks and arranged the food on the table. Without ostentation, he pulled out her chair for her, then sat down opposite.

Jenny bit into her hamburger, thinking nothing had ever tasted so good. She should never have gone all day without a proper meal, but Blackie's arrival at the restaurant had upset her routine and thrown her off balance. The accident had been the last straw.

"You don't have to pay me a salary,'' he said, making inroads on the onion rings.

"To quote you, it would look very strange if you didn't collect a paycheck like everyone else. Or does a journalist make a much better living than the rest of the world realizes?''

A mysterious glint came and went in his eyes. "We manage to eke out a living. How about you restaurant managers?''

CHAPTER THREE

JENNY ALMOST CHOKED on the last of her hamburger and reached quickly for a drink. "We survive."

One dark brow quirked. "Does everyone around here call you Ms. Connelly?"

"No. We're an informal bunch. My name's Jenny."

He smiled. "An old-fashioned name for a modern woman. I like it. I like you, Jenny Connelly."

"You've landed the job, Mr. Blackwell. You don't have to lay on the charm to stay on my good side."

His smile deepened. "I'll keep that in mind. But my name's Blackie, remember?"

"And very apropos it is. How could I forget a name that sounds like a third-rate villain out of a sixth-rate western novel?" she drawled.

He flashed her an indecipherable glance. "I take it you don't like westerns."

"Westerns, romances, mysteries. Most of them are chloroform in print." She didn't really believe that, but said it just to see Blackie's reaction. She vaguely remembered a column he'd written about the value of popular fiction. It was one her father had drawn to her attention. At the time, she'd been surprised by the famous Corbin Blackwell's unpretentious acceptance of stories written purely for the sake of entertainment.

And now, if his scowl was anything to go by, she'd hit a tiny nerve. Perversely, that pleased her.

"Don't tell me you're one of those people who believe the only worthwhile literature is found in the classics?"

"Don't be so touchy, Blackie. My father certainly considered *your* writing worthwhile, not only for the clarity of your style, but your insights."

"That's gratifying to know. But I'm more interested in hearing what his daughter thinks."

Jenny took her time answering. "I was afraid you'd ask that question. The truth is, I haven't been an avid newspaper reader for quite some time." Certainly not since her escapades had been sensationalized in the gossip columns.

"At least you're honest," he said with a good-natured grin, making her feel more uncomfortable. "Now that we've finished dinner, how about fulfilling one of my fantasies and going for a ride with me on my motorcycle? I always envied the guy who roared down the highway with a gorgeous woman behind him, her hands tight around his waist and her beautiful long legs tucked right next to his." He glanced meaningfully at her own shapely limbs with their Southern California tan, and instantly her face went hot.

"Don't even men named Blackie know it's not polite to oogle a woman?"

"Oogle?" he repeated with a bark of laughter.

"That's what my father used to call it," she reminisced with a small smile of her own.

"I'm not sure that word's in any dictionary I've ever consulted, but when a woman has legs as exquisite as yours, even a saint crumbles under the strain. So you can imagine how hard it is on us Blackies.''

"Well, saint or sinner, I'm afraid you're going to be disappointed, because I don't ride around on motorcycles in shorts." At least not anymore, she amended to herself.

His mouth quirked ever so slightly. "Why don't we compromise? If you'll come off your high horse long enough to go riding with me dressed as you are, I promise to keep my attention fastened on your glorious hair. To help you preserve your dignity,'' he added playfully.

She darted him a fiery glance. "That would be rather difficult to do unless I was the one driving, don't you think?''

"Now that's a thought.'' His eyes glimmered with amusement. No doubt he was recalling her accident and wouldn't dream of letting her touch the controls.

"You don't think I could do it, do you?" She'd dated a boy in high school who'd taught her how to ride his Kawasaki. Until they'd broken up, he'd let her take it everywhere. That was when she'd talked her father into buying her one.

His eyes narrowed a fraction. "Somehow you don't seem the type.''

"Neither do you.'' She flashed him a guileless smile. "But it just goes to show you can't judge a book by its cover." She practically gagged on the ghastly cliché, but the look of puzzlement in his eyes was worth it. "I have a motorcycle back home in the garage. I drove it when I was a teenager, but I passed through that stage years ago.''

"The next time you go back, why not bring it with you? We can ride around in the desert after work. By the way, where is home?"

"Santa Barbara." She decided she'd better stick to the truth whenever possible because one day everyone at O'Brien's would know she was the principal shareholder. But not yet. She still had a long way to go to prove herself first.

He eyed her intently. "Out of all the places you might have picked to work, how did you happen to come here, Jenny?"

She chewed slowly on a leftover french fry, and she thought about everything Vi Allen had done for her. "Well, I decided to learn about the restaurant business, and this friend of mine told me Tom was a good person to work for and would teach me the ropes. I called him and he told me I could start to train as long as I was willing to live in one of these trailers. He, uh, said he couldn't have me going back and forth to Santa Barbara all the time."

"That makes sense." He finished his drink. "What did you do before that?"

She'd been afraid of that question. "I lived with my father, went to school, worked a little. But he's gone now." To her dismay, her voice caught and her eyes filled with tears.

There was a charged silence in the trailer. "I take it he died recently."

She nodded without looking up. "A couple of months ago. The house felt like a tomb, so I decided to get out and do something different. You know...to stand on my own two feet. What about you? Your speech is almost foreign compared to our western twang, but I can't believe you're a native New Yorker, either.''

There was a distinct pause. "You're right, so why don't you guess?''

She cocked her head. "You don't sound like the Kennedys, so that rules out Massachusetts. Maybe Vermont, New Hampshire, Maine?''

The blue of his eyes deepened. She'd hit the jackpot with one of them, anyway. "You have a good ear. I was born in Newport, Vermont.''

She'd never heard of it. "You're a long way from home, Blackie.''

He shifted his weight, drawing her attention to his lean powerful build. "I know. So humor me on my first night in a strange place and keep me company.''

He was temptation itself, but Jenny knew better than to spend any more time with this man, except on the job. "I'm sorry, but I have to work on the books tonight. Why don't you go over to the museum and take a look around?''

"I did that this afternoon." He sounded as though he was very aware she was trying to avoid him. "Well, since I can't persuade you to go for a ride with me, maybe I'll head back to my trailer and get some writing done.''

"How do you handle the pressure of turning out a weekly column and working another job under cover at the same time?'' she couldn't refrain from asking.

"I submit my columns as much as two months ahead of deadline. Since they usually don't focus on headline issues, it's not a problem.''

"So I have to wait that long to see what you're going to write about us?''

"You're welcome to look at my rough drafts any-time," he offered with a definite gleam in his eye. To her consternation, a wave of heat suffused her face. "I think I'm going to do my next feature on redheads," he said with a chuckle. "I'll explore whether there's a correlation between the intensity of hair color and the sudden change in skin tone. Do fiery redheads blush more often than say, strawberry blondes?"

Her lips curved into a full unguarded smile. "I don't imagine the public would be all that interested in your findings."

He stared at her for a long moment. "I'm one of the public, and since coming to the desert, I've found the subject fascinates me." He reached abruptly for some paperbacks sitting on a shelf by the table and examined the titles. "I thought you didn't like popular fiction."

"If you recall, I said *most* fiction. But I have to admit I'm a fan of Ludlum and Boyd."

"Mind if I borrow one? I don't have any reading material yet." He tucked the top book under his arm.

"Be my guest," she said through gritted teeth. "But I'm surprised you haven't read them. I thought every red-blooded American male had devoured the lot."

He slanted her a brief unfathomable glance. "Writing consumes a great deal of my time and doesn't leave much room to indulge in reading for pure enjoyment." He moved toward the door of her trailer. "I'll return this in a day or two. What time did you say I was to report for work in the morning?"

"Seven."

"Who's going to teach me how to wash dishes?"

Jenny swallowed hard. "I am."

His eyes twinkled with devilment. "Your penance for hiring me, I'll wager. And here I thought I was going to be left to my own devices for the duration. Something tells me we're going to make a terrific team."

As she sat there wondering how long she could resist his charm, he studied her intently and said, "I can see you agree with me."

"I don't know, Blackie. Washing dishes eight hours a day is deadly. I hope you don't have a back problem."

"Not as far as I know. What about you? I hope carrying you in here didn't make you too uncomfortable."

"I don't remember," she said quickly. "I was still shaking with reaction."

He raised one eyebrow and said only, "I'll see you in the morning." Then he was gone and to her chagrin had taken the newest L. E. Boyd mystery with him. She'd been looking forward to starting it that night. When she didn't hear his motorcycle, she went over to the window and saw him entering the trailer next door.

Was it coincidence that with several vacant trailers on the lot, he was put in the one next to hers? If today was any indication, Blackie Archer would be insinuating himself into her life, no matter where she turned.

What really frightened her was that he was right about the magic. She could feel a certain tension, an awareness between them. It was something that had never happened to her before. Frowning at the trend of her thoughts, she pulled out the restaurant account books and tried to immerse herself in profit-and-loss statements, but visions of working with Blackie kept sending a thrill of excitement through her body.

When her alarm went off at six the next morning, Jenny threw off her covers and hurried into the shower to get ready for work. She felt the same sense of expectancy and eagerness she'd experienced the night before, but she was reluctant to admit these feelings had anything to do with Blackie.

He was Corbin Blackwell the journalist, and this dishwashing job was only a temporary cover until he'd finished his research. She had no intention of getting involved with a man who'd be gone in a few weeks, a man who'd forget her the minute he met someone else—someone whose help he needed with the next research project. As he needed *her* help with this one.

The restaurant was full of truckers and tourists when she walked in half an hour later dressed in a cotton skirt and blouse. Despite the crowd, her attention went immediately to Blackie, who sat on a stool at the counter, talking to Sharlene, one of the waitresses.

Whatever he was saying caused Sharlene, an attractive thirty-five-year-old who looked twenty-five, to respond with animation. Blackie had made his first conquest of the morning simply by passing the time of day with the woman while he had breakfast. Sharlene could be forgiven if she had no idea of his true intentions.

Glad he was occupied, Jenny slipped into the kitchen for a piece of toast and juice, then went to her office to check the daily roster and deal with any notes in the input box.

At five to seven she returned to the dining room and signaled Blackie to follow her. Even from the distance separating them, she saw the flicker of recognition in his blue eyes. Immediately he stood up and followed her into the kitchen.

She introduced him to everyone, from the chefs to the busboys. Male and female staff alike seemed happy to have Blackie aboard, reacting favorably to his warmth and his sense of humor. In no time at all, he'd have enough information to fill a file cabinet.

Jenny avoided Blackie's covert glances as they put on the loose green jackets worn by O'Brien's employees for scraping dishes and placing them on the conveyer belt that fed into the dishwasher.

"What do you think?" Blackie forced her to look at him when he'd finished buttoning up.

"What can I say?" she said with an exaggerated shrug. "Put a man in uniform and he has the world at his feet."

His mouth twitched in amusement. "That's the basic difference between the sexes. It doesn't matter what a woman wears."

Jenny should have been used to his banter by now, but for once she couldn't think of a comeback. Her face probably matched the red of her hair. "Are you ready to tackle that mound of dishes waiting for you in the corner?"

His gaze followed the direction of her head movement, and he grimaced. "If you're trying to frighten me, you've succeeded admirably."

She laughed. "You've never been frightened in your life!" She leaned over to adjust the slim buckle on one of her sandals. "Let's get started, shall we?" she added brusquely.

"I've been waiting to hear you say that," he said in a low voice. "Don't you think there's something kind of homey about doing dishes together?"

"Have you ever washed dishes in a restaurant before?"

"No." He grinned. "But something tells me I'm about to."

Her arm brushed his accidentally as she passed in front of him, headed for the dishwashing area. The brief contact left her trembling, and she moved ahead quickly so there'd be no recurrence.

"Sharlene says it's exhausting work for the first little while. We'll probably need to take a break later. How about going for a ride on the bike?" he murmured near her ear.

"I hate to disappoint you, Blackie, but your first break isn't until nine, and it's only for ten minutes, not long enough to go anywhere."

"Then have coffee with me." His challenge floated sensuously over her shoulder.

"I think right now you'd better concentrate on work." She proceeded to give him his first lesson in washing dishes. Showing Blackie the ropes was a novel experience. For the first twenty minutes she made suggestions and pointed out more efficient ways to stack plates and cups as she watched his progress.

"You're beginning to sound like my editor," he said. "He's a perfectionist, too."

Jenny couldn't restrain a smile. "You're quite the diplomat when it suits you."

He eyed her over the conveyor belt. "Will I dash that image irrevocably if I ask you a personal question?"

"I suppose it depends on the question."

"Is there a man in your life?"

Jenny glanced at the silverware she was sorting, hoping he couldn't tell how much the switch of topics surprised her. For a moment she wanted to believe he'd asked her that question because of a personal interest in her, an attraction. But then sanity returned. He was a journalist out to gather material for his columns. It was his only reason for being at O'Brien's.

"No, there's not. What about you?" she said in an even voice.

"Not now. I was married—once."

Jenny schooled her features to betray no reaction, but she was mentally calculating that since he'd checked the box marked "single" on his application form, and not the "divorced" box, it meant his wife had died. Still in mourning for her father, she felt compassion for Blackie's loss and it prompted her to ask, "Was she a journalist, too?"

He shook his head. "We were high-school sweethearts and got married after graduation. There was a hotel fire where we were spending out honeymoon. We were overcome by smoke, and by the time help arrived Helen was too far gone. She died on the way to the hospital." The tremor in his voice told her more than words how deeply the loss had affected him.

Jenny's hands stilled. She didn't know what to say. To have lost his bride in such a cruel way must have scarred him for life. She couldn't imagine ever getting over something like that. Perhaps this tragedy explained his need to live on the edge, to stay on the move. Perhaps it had created a restlessness in him, a restlessness that took him from one place to the next in search of stories—and away from memories?

"Jenny," he called softly over the conveyor belt. "I shouldn't have told you if you're going to go all teary-eyed on me. The doctors swore she suffered no pain. That made all the difference, and eventually I was able to get on with my life—which, right now, is looking better and better."

She whispered how sorry she was, inwardly wondering how he'd been able to pick up the pieces and go on. It put her father's death in a different perspective.

"Hey," he called to her again. "If I'd known how this was going to affect you, I wouldn't have told you. It happened a lifetime ago."

"It must have been so painful, Blackie. To lose her before you'd had the opportunity to have a life together... I can't imagine surviving that kind of pain."

"At the time, I couldn't imagine it, either. But youth is resilient. I should know—I'm living proof." His sweet smile broke through her defenses.

"I'm glad you got on with your life. Corbin Blackwell has made a lasting impact on the American scene."

His expression sobered. "I thought you didn't read my column."

She let out a shaky breath. "My father quoted you regularly."

"You thought a lot of your father, didn't you?"

She couldn't dispel the lump lodged in her throat. "Yes. In some ways, he was larger than life."

"You haven't mentioned your mother."

"She died when I was little."

There was a moment's pause, and she felt his eyes intent on her face. "So your dad raised you alone?"

She nodded but didn't break her rhythm while she loaded glasses. Right now would be the perfect time to tell him the truth, that Donald O'Brien was her father. She felt guilty keeping her identity a secret when she knew *his* identity and when he'd told her so much about himself. But she couldn't say anything until she'd told Tom first.

"No brothers or sisters?"

"No." Jenny shook her head, more and more uncomfortable with his questions. "What about you?" she asked quickly.

He was busy arranging water glasses on the rack. Amazingly, he seemed to be a natural at everything he did. "I have two sisters, both of whom are married with families."

At this point she felt like shouting at him to stop talking because she knew exactly what he was doing, what he was after. This wasn't working out at all. In far too short a time he'd managed to make her care about him. He was becoming important to her. Every time she looked up, there he was, smiling, too clever by far, so handsome it was hard to concentrate on anything else.

"You seem to be doing well, Blackie. I'm going to leave you on your own for a little while but I'll be back," she said briskly, giving him a professional smile before walking off. A slight nod was his only response, but she couldn't help wondering if he'd instinctively recognized the real reason for her sudden departure.

Breathing a little easier now that she was away from him, she made her rounds of the restaurant, then came back to the kitchen after his break and worked with him until noon. Not that he needed her supervision any longer, as Sharlene was quick to point out with a knowing smile. Nothing got past Sharlene.

And she was right of course! While Jenny was occupied with other responsibilities, Blackie had developed an expertise for the job that shouldn't have surprised her.

"Where do you think you're going?" He caught up with her when it was time to go to lunch. Little did he know her back was in pain from standing in one position for two hours, and she longed to lie down. Dishwashers weren't paid half enough in her opinion. She planned to remedy the situation one day. What irked her most was that Blackie seemed perfectly happy and hadn't complained once about anything!

"I'm going to my trailer to put in some more work on the books. I'll be back when you start the afternoon shift."

"Since you weren't around for our coffee break, I was hoping we could eat together."

She fought to keep her voice steady, impersonal. "You said you wanted to find out what went on behind the scenes at O'Brien's. Now's your opportunity. Don't forget we're having dinner with Tom and Marva tonight. Seven o'clock."

"I haven't forgotten," he whispered, implying an intimacy all out of proportion to the situation.

"GOOD NIGHT, Marva, Tom. Thanks again for everything. See you in the morning." Blackie ushered Jenny out of the restaurant, his hand resting on the small of her back in a proprietary manner. Several truckers watched their progress with interest, but Jenny hardly noticed. Her mind was on the evening they'd just spent.

She hadn't missed the silent messages passing between Tom and Marva expressing their delight at having such a prominent person in their employ—however temporary the arrangement. When Tom smiled directly at Jenny, she beamed back as if nothing in the world was bothering her, but inside she was a mass of troubled emotions.

Marva had been as warm and friendly as Tom. She'd plied Blackie with hundreds of questions Jenny had been dying to ask him. Blackie had a way of enchanting his audience, and she could have listened to his experiences until far into the night. Interestingly enough, it was Blackie who made the excuse that he'd had a long day and needed to get to bed.

A hot desert breeze filled the silk flounce on Jenny's soft peach-colored blouse as they walked toward Blackie's motorcycle. She'd purposely worn this outfit with its matching full skirt so that sitting astride the bike wouldn't be a problem. She fervently hoped he wouldn't suggest she drive. Those days were over.

The sun had gone down, but the western sky still made her breath catch with its glorious display of crimson and gold.

"Dear Lord, you're beautiful," Blackie whispered. "Right this second your hair looks like it's on fire and the silvery flecks inside the darker rim of your irises are shimmering like tiny crystals. I wish I was an artist so I could capture you on canvas.''

In the ever-changing wonder of the sun's rays, he looked rather spectacular himself, she thought, but she could never have been as articulate or poetic. Had Blackie spoken as the writer, or did the words flow naturally? Where did the role-playing end? At what point did the real person take over?

Whoever he was right now, she saw as many varying shades of blue in his eyes as in the darkening sky to the east. The cleft in his strong chin was more pronounced. So was his well-defined mouth. Looking at it made her feel a quickening inside as she imagined it on hers.

The night's magic seemed to have woven its spell around Blackie, too. She knew she was playing a dangerous game even being out here with him. Right now her heart was pounding so hard it threatened to suffocate her.

The smell of sage and sand, the wonderful scent of his hair and skin, all mingled with her own perfume to fill her senses with longings as old as time. Several tendrils of her hair brushed against his smooth-shaven cheek. He caught the strands around his finger and held them just tight enough to prevent her from moving away.

''Let's take a ride.'' The thickness of his voice sent an answering shiver through her body. She thought he'd been serious when he made his excuses to Tom and Marva. Now she knew why he'd insisted on leaving. Hesitantly, she followed his lead. She couldn't seem to help herself.

Sitting behind him, she wrapped her arms around his waist as he turned on the ignition and revved the engine. He felt warm and solid. He felt good, so good she wanted to press herself against his back, but she quelled the instinct.

Once he'd maneuvered through the semis and tankers to the highway, they headed for the trailer park. She didn't question where they were going; words seemed unnecessary. She threw back her head to gaze at the sky as he took a bike path behind the trailers and rode toward the open desert.

She sighed in wonder at a sliver of moon with Venus in its crescent and at the stars just beginning to appear in the royal-blue canopy above the horizon. Blackie must have been equally moved by the beauty of the heavens because he slowed to a stop. They both got off the bike and stood together savoring the moment.

"Why would a person want to work anywhere else when he could be a part of *this* every night?" At the sound of his voice Jenny turned her head and discovered him gazing down at her with an unmistakable message in his eyes. Somehow he'd managed to trap her between his arms. Her back was against the motorcycle and she couldn't move without stepping right into his embrace.

She kept telling herself she'd walked into this situation with her eyes wide open. But there was an excitement about him, a pure male aura that drew her inexorably toward him. "You took the words right out of my mouth, Blackie."

She heard his sharp intake of breath. "I'd like to do a lot more than that. You can believe it or not, but I've never in my life felt the power of a woman's magic so quickly.''

''This is a new experience for me, too. I think I'm a little frightened by my response to you.'' The scary part of her admission was that it was absolutely true.

''You should be,'' he said on a deadly serious note that could mean any number of things.

Suddenly she felt a need to lighten the mood between them. She forced herself to meet his gaze with a teasing smile. ''Is the famous Corbin Blackwell really a notorious murderer on the loose? Is that why you call yourself Blackie?'' Her bravado hid the trembling inside her.

To her surprise, he paled visibly in the emerging starlight. A physical reaction like that was impossible to fake. She couldn't imagine what had caused it.

''If I were a wanted man, you'd be helpless. We're several miles from civilization. No one would hear you cry out. Didn't you think of that before you agreed to go for a ride with me?'' he asked in a tense voice.

''Poor Blackie.'' She put a hand on his forearm. ''Have you been on the move for so long you've forgotten a little thing called trust? I think maybe you're more afraid than I am or we wouldn't be talking right now.'' She delighted in goading him. Because she had no expectation that their relationship would go anywhere, Jenny felt she could indulge in a little teasing.

''You don't know what you're talking about.''

''I think I do,'' she said gently. ''A roving reporter can't afford to be tied down too long in one place,'' she continued, eyeing him from beneath her long lashes. ''I can understand your caution, Blackie. Particularly when we'll be spending most of our working hours together until you move on, and there's nothing much to do when we're off duty.''

''Lady,'' he muttered gruffly, ''you couldn't be more wrong.'' Hot blue flames of desire leapt in his eyes, scorching her as he lowered his dark head and blotted out the moon, the stars, the very night with his kiss.

There was nothing tentative about the way his mouth crushed hers, probing, demanding until she gave a tiny moan of pleasure. Then she helplessly began to kiss him back, marveling at the sensations his lips aroused. Tremor after tremor shook her body, yet the only point of contact was his mouth on hers.

When Jenny realized she wanted to be wrapped in his arms, she pulled away, breaking off a kiss that had apparently affected him every bit as much as her. His head reared back and his breathing was shallow, as if he'd been running a great distance.

His eyes feasted on her face, examining every flushed feature, the redness of her vulnerable mouth. ''We're in serious trouble. I guess you know that.''

She knew, but would rather die than admit it. ''Don't read too much into it, Blackie. I've kissed other men with equal pleasure. The fact is, you're here to do a story, and when you have what you came for, you'll be gone. It would be better to take it slow and easy. You know what I mean.''

She could tell she'd irritated him, because he shifted his weight and a mask seemed to come down over his face. ''How do you know I won't take root right here? Maybe it's time this old man stopped globe-trotting. I have a good steady job, plenty of food, a roof over my head, and a woman—who looks like the stuff a man's dreams are made of—living right next door.''

''It would grow old fast, Blackie, and then the journalist would take over and you'd be off to parts unknown for another story.'' She had to say it out loud, if only to convince herself.

Mentioning his research seemed to trigger something in Blackie, because he withdrew and swung one leg over the motorcycle seat. ''Slow and easy?'' he mocked, casting her an ironic glance over his shoulder as she climbed on behind him. ''I wonder who's going to regret that statement more?''

They rode back to the trailer park in silence. Jenny slipped off the seat the moment he came to a full stop. She gave him the benefit of her most demure smile. ''Thank you for the ride, Blackie. I'll see you at seven in the morning.''

He sat astride his cycle with his gaze fastened on her mouth. The way he was looking at her, he might as well have been kissing her again. She wished he would, with a longing that was as painful as it was unfamiliar. He knew exactly what he was doing to her, and worse, he knew how it was making her feel. ''Good night, Jenny.''

She hurried into her trailer and locked the door, not trusting herself any more than she trusted him. She fought the temptation to look out the window until she'd showered and prepared for bed.

His light was still on, which meant he was probably recording his observations for the day. Or maybe he was reading her book, the one she wished she had right now. But on second thought, she doubted she'd have been able to concentrate on the story. Too much had happened since Blackie had arrived in the Mojave.

Jenny felt as though she was living another life now, and it was Blackie's fault. But a nagging voice whispered that she'd ignored the warnings and gone willingly into his arms. She'd forgotten all sense of caution when he kissed her. She shouldn't have allowed it. She'd thought she could handle the situation, but before she finally fell asleep, she had the horrible premonition that he'd outmaneuvered her from the beginning.

New tactics were called for if she was to avoid getting hurt. Allowing their relationship to develop would only bring pain. Temporary involvement with a woman would mean little to a man like Blackie; it probably went with the territory. But one kiss had colored Jenny's world. No, it couldn't go on. And the approach that made the most sense was to keep things on a strictly professional basis until he left O'Brien's. Six long weeks from now.

CHAPTER FOUR

WHEN JENNY ENTERED the dining room the next morning she saw Blackie monopolizing not only Sharlene but several of the other waitresses, who stood clustered around him. Naturally he was on the job, charming information out of each of them in his captivating way.

Her first instinct was to slip into the kitchen unnoticed and eat breakfast. But then it occurred to her that Blackie had probably planned this little scene. He didn't like Jenny's suggestion about taking their relationship slow and easy, so he intended to make her jealous. In order to do that, he had to speed things up—and what better way than to flirt with the other female employees?

Inhaling a breath of fresh determination, Jenny made her way to the counter and eased onto the stool next to him. She had to let him know she was immune to that kind of ploy. And she had to persuade him she really wasn't interested in the kind of casual fling he expected.

He was dressed in hip-hugging jeans and a T-shirt Tom had designed for the snake museum. The front had a caricature of a granddaddy rattler, and on the back was a caption that read "Give your snake an O'Brien break."

Jenny started to laugh. She couldn't help it. "Good morning, Blackie. I called for you but when you didn't answer, I assumed you were still asleep. Now I can see I was wrong. Tom'll love you forever." She ran her hand lightly across the back of his shirt.

A smile of understanding transformed his features, making him far too attractive this early in the day. He put down his coffee cup and turned in her direction, his gaze wandering to her hair, which was caught in a loose knot to keep it out of the way. The style emphasized the delicate bone structure of her face.

"I like it," he murmured.

"Thank you." The simple compliment shouldn't have shaken her; but it was hard to be immune to the combination of his deep voice and the glimmer of admiration in his eyes.

"As a matter of fact, I came by for you, too, but got no answer, so I decided to let Sleeping Beauty dream on."

His technique was flawless. "I was probably in the shower."

"I can tell. You smell divine. Is it your hair or your skin or the perfume you wear? Whatever it is, it's dynamite."

She suspected that the full complement of flattering remarks meant he was following his battle plan religiously. His innate charm made all the people he came in contact with feel so special and important they found themselves telling him anything he wanted to know. She wondered, almost bitterly, how many women had fallen in love with him as he courted and cajoled them in the name of research. She wondered how many hearts he'd left broken in various parts of the world. As for his own heart, it had probably been buried with his wife.

"Now, how come he didn't say anything like that to me?" Sharlene piped up, smiling at the two of them as she poured water for Jenny.

"Because you're not the boss," Jenny supplied easily. "Blackie's trying to stay on my good side."

"I'm working on it," he whispered for her hearing alone.

Sharlene noticed the byplay and grinned at Jenny. "What'll you have?"

"I think orange juice and toast."

"So that's how you keep your figure." She winked without a trace of malice. "Do you see what working here for five years has done to me?" She patted her hips, covered by the green skirt, but as far as Jenny could tell, Sharlene didn't have anything to worry about.

"I'd say five years here agrees with you beautifully, Sharlene," Blackie said in a sincere voice.

"Oh, go on." She laughed as if she'd heard that line a thousand times before. "You'd better watch out for him," she teased, looking at Jenny as she filled the salt and pepper shakers. "This character's dangerous, and I mean with a capital *D*." She raised her pale eyebrows as if to emphasize her point and walked off to place Jenny's order with the kitchen.

Luckily Jenny had her glass of water and drinking it hid her answering smile. She supposed Sharlene had been around men in this business for so long she could spot a phony a mile away. She had to admire the other woman's finesse and her pleasant disposition. Tom had nominated Sharlene for waitress of the year and

Jenny could see why. Rule number one for a good waitress was to brush off remarks from the merely provocative to the crude, and still come up smiling.

Jenny turned to Blackie. "I saw your light on when I went to bed. Were you writing or reading?" As a general rule, Jenny found that when people talked about their favorite authors, they could go on for hours. She was determined to keep things light.

For the briefest moment he seemed preoccupied by her question, but maybe she was only imagining it. "Normally I can write any time. But last night a certain redhead kept interfering with my concentration, so I finally gave up. Getting involved in a book was equally impossible."

"I'm serious." She was trying desperately to avoid anything personal between them.

"So am I," came the solemn response. She bit her lip in frustration. The conversation wasn't going as she'd planned, and worse, her heart had started its ridiculous hammering.

"Daddy loved Boyd's mysteries. That's how I got hooked on them." She reached for the orange juice Sharlene placed in front of her and drank it as if she'd been dying of thirst. As for the toast, she didn't think she could eat it, after all.

As soon as Sharlene had refilled his coffee cup and moved on to a customer, Blackie turned toward Jenny, giving her his full attention. "Your father had discriminating taste. As a matter of fact, I like them, too. I also enjoy baseball, German cars, Brahms, rhubarb pie and luscious-looking redheads, not necessarily in that order. Now it's your turn."

"Sorry to disappoint you, but it's seven o'clock and time for work."

"That's good because I want to talk to you about last night."

"I can't imagine why."

"Liar," he whispered before they took up positions on opposite sides of the conveyor belt. "You looked as dazed as I was. I've kissed a few women in my time, but my experience with you made me feel like I'd been run over by one of those huge semis parked out front."

She paused in her scraping. "Unfortunately I always feel like that when a man kisses me, so I try not to let it happen very often."

"You shouldn't have told me that. It makes me want to find out what it would be like to kiss you without a motorcycle hampering my style."

Ignoring his reference to the night before, she said, "I'll leave you by yourself for a while and go to my office. If you have any problems—though I'm sure you won't—come and get me."

"That sounds suspiciously like you're trying to get away from me," he said dryly. "I have news for you, sweetheart. Your office won't protect you. You're well and truly stuck with me, morning, noon and night."

"Except when I take my long weekends," she retorted.

"I've been thinking about that." His blue eyes sent her a private message. "Let's go together. I'd like to spend time with you at the ocean."

"We don't have the same days off."

"I'll talk to Tom and see if it can't be arranged."

"Have you made some kind of deal I don't know about?" She gazed at him with what she hoped was an intimidating expression.

"Men have their own fraternity when it comes to women. He'll understand."

Her eyes closed involuntarily. Tom was so taken with Blackie he'd probably agree to anything.

"Let's have a picnic lunch out on the desert today," he said softly.

Her eyes flew open. "Sorry. I'm working through my lunch hour."

Lines darkened his face. "I don't believe you. Why are you starting to avoid me, Jenny?"

"Whatever gave you that idea?" He was too perceptive by far.

"Don't pretend with me."

"I'm not pretending."

He moved around to her side of the conveyor belt and stood close, examining her flushed face. "Then prove it by going out with me tonight."

She swallowed hard as a strange little pain ran from her fingers to every part of her body. "Maybe after work we could drive into Barstow and see a movie."

The town of approximately 17,000 in San Bernardino County was fifty miles from O'Brien's. She'd passed through it dozens of times in the early hours of the morning, always on her way to somewhere else. Now she'd said the first thing that came to mind because she was fast losing control of the situation. And because she desperately wanted to escape to the solitude of her office.

"In lieu of being together now?" he asked with maddening persistence.

"Why don't you ask Sharlene to eat with you if you're that lonely?"

"Sharlene doesn't have red hair." Jenny started to leave the kitchen but he was right on her heels. "I'll be ready to go whenever you say the word."

She did some mental calculating. "I should be off duty by six-thirty at the latest."

His facial muscles relaxed. "Now that I know we have a date for this evening, I'm looking forward to getting through the rest of the day's work."

She paused before leaving the kitchen. "We'd better take the truck. It'll be too hot to ride your motorcycle."

"You don't mind?"

"Of course not."

"Just for that, I'll let you pick the movie."

"You might be sorry."

"I'll take my chances."

"Don't say I didn't warn you." She smiled mischievously and hurried off to do her work. But if she thought she could keep thoughts of Blackie from intruding on her consciousness, she was wrong. As the day wore on, her anticipation grew, and she was almost sick with excitement by the time they finally drove away from the trailer court and headed to Barstow.

THIS WAS THE FIRST time she'd found herself driving Barstow's hot streets at ten in the evening with a man she'd only known three days.

Upon arriving in town, Blackie had insisted they visit the local garage first, to make arrangements for repairing the damage to her front fender. The garage had lent her another truck until hers was repaired, for which Jenny was grateful. She had a vintage Porsche at home in Santa Barbara but wouldn't have flaunted it in front of the staff.

She'd purposely left the car behind, under the watchful eye of the Riveras, the couple who'd always looked after the house. The last thing she wanted was to draw undue attention to herself. She'd had a surfeit of notoriety for more years than she cared to remember.

Now she was attached to her dad's pickup, if only for sentimental reasons, and appreciated Blackie's concern that it be repaired as quickly as possible.

She wouldn't have brought her dad's Cadillac any more than her Porsche. They were still parked side by side in the garage at home. She couldn't bear to part with any of his things. He'd loved that particular car. He'd loved everything American and said that the country would never achieve economic greatness until Americans started buying American products.

Yet he'd bought her the restored 356 Porsche as a twenty-first birthday present because he knew she was crazy about it. He used to tease her that it looked like a bathtub, but that was one of the reasons she loved it. That and the fact that it was a speedster and hugged the road superbly as it wound along the coastal highway through the Big Sur. Occasionally she'd been able to talk her dad into going for a ride, but he always insisted it added more gray hairs to his head.

"You're deep in thought," Blackie said to her now. "I hope you're not going to have nightmares tonight." He hadn't taken his eyes off her while they filled up at the gas station before heading home. What he didn't know, and what she hated to admit even to herself, was that she could hardly take her eyes off him, either.

He wore white trousers and a navy silk shirt that looked Italian in design and feel. Tonight he was the cosmopolitan sophisticate. And infinitely desirable.

As he'd left the choice of film up to her—and there wasn't much of a choice, since between them, she and Blackie had already seen almost every movie in town—she decided to annoy him by picking an absurd horror show. To her amazement, he'd acted as if he enjoyed it, and he'd managed to frighten her once or twice during the scary parts by growling into her neck. Then he'd made amends by feeding her popcorn. She couldn't tell if it was accidental or not that his fingers made frequent contact with her lips.

All she knew was that she was glad when the film had finally come to an end. He'd been whispering to her, touching her all evening long, and it had to stop.

"If that's a hint you'd be willing to spend the night with me, then you're even more predictable than the plot of that ghastly film."

"You mean you knew the girl was going to get it when she ran out into the woods in her nightgown in the middle of the night with no one around for miles?" He chuckled seductively.

"You noticed."

"What would really scare you?" he asked on a more solemn note.

"I once saw *Dr. Jekyll and Mr. Hyde*. It was the version with Spencer Tracy. There was something terrifying about the way he changed. In fact, the villain in this story reminded me a bit of Jekyll and Hyde. I suppose the idea of a human being having two personalities in one body frightens me as much as anything.''

''That's very interesting.'' He rubbed the back of his neck, sounding far away. ''Psychotic killers have always fascinated me, as well. They're totally unpredictable. That's what makes them so terrifying. Some small thing will set them off. I spent time at a maximum-security prison interviewing some killers once. They're a strange breed.''

Jenny shivered at the direction their conversation had taken. ''Could we change the subject?''

''What's the matter? Are you afraid to be alone in the dark with me?'' He sounded like Bela Lugosi, the actor who'd played the first Count Dracula.

''Blackie!'' she cried when he leaned across from the passenger seat and pretended to bite her neck. The feel of his lips against her skin made her shiver again, for a different reason this time.

He slid back to his side of the truck. ''All right. I'll leave you alone, but only until we reach the trailer park.''

She took a shaky breath. ''I'll get a headache if I stay up any later.''

''You can't have another headache,'' he said, and she could almost feel his smile. ''You're only allowed one per day, and you've already used up your quota. You'll have to think up another excuse.''

''I don't need one. Six o'clock comes awfully early.''

''You're right. Wouldn't it be simpler if we just pulled off the road somewhere and spent the night in the open instead of driving all the way back to the trailers to sleep alone? Look at the stars, Jenny. Just look at them!''

She *had* looked at them. But when she'd accidentally caught a glimpse of herself in the rearview mirror, she'd seen stars in her eyes that had outshone those in the heavens. Something was happening to her. Something so disturbing she didn't dare explore it for fear of what she'd discover.

''The truck floor leaves a lot to be desired, Blackie. It could give a person back problems.''

''I'd willingly go into traction for the chance to spend a night in your arms.''

''I think I'll need traction after another morning of washing dishes with you.''

''I can remedy your back pains, Jenny. For a while I was a physical therapist in a hospital.''

''Yes, I remember. Was that so you could do more research?''

''That's right. It was a rehabilitation hospital for members of the CIA who'd been wounded in the line of duty. I was doing a story on them.''

''You mean like in the James Bond movie where Sean Connery gets locked in the sauna and left to die? Was it like that?''

She felt him take a deep breath. ''Exactly like that.''

''How thrilling!'' He was quiet so long she thought he'd gone to sleep. ''Blackie?''

''What?''

''Tell me more.''

''Why do I get the feeling you're patronizing me?''

She accelerated to pass a driver who was doing fifty-five. Actually she'd been perfectly content to travel at that speed since leaving Barstow, but hearing about

Blackie's research reminded her of the reason he'd come to the desert. One day soon he'd have accomplished his objective, and he'd be gone. She was in danger of forgetting that important fact.

"My charms must be fading. I've never put a woman to sleep at the wheel before," he mumbled wryly.

She broke her concentration to glance at him. "You'll never be in danger of doing that, Blackie. Tell me about your family. Do you ever take time out to visit them? How do they feel about you gallivanting all over the world?"

His face darkened, and she thought he looked like an avenging prince when the headlights of a car illuminated him for a second. "My family came to grips with it years ago. I spend every Christmas with them. Any other questions?"

"You don't need to be so touchy. I'm only trying to understand the less public side of the famous Corbin Blackwell. After you've left O'Brien's, it'll be fun to tell people you used to work for us. Tom thinks you're more of a celebrity than Howard Hughes, and that's saying a lot!"

She heard a muttered imprecation as his arm moved against the back of the cab seat so that his fingers were agonizingly close to her neck. "You sound like you can't wait to get rid of me. Apparently my celebrity status doesn't impress you. Are you trying to tell me I'm not in the running?" For once he sounded angry.

"Please don't take this wrong, Blackie, but when I bumped into you the day before yesterday and then found out who you were and why you'd come to O'Brien's, I have to admit I was disappointed."

"In what way?" His voice was quiet but alert.

"I suppose I have a dream that most women share. To meet a man who looks like you, of course, but has a good nine-to-five job and hurries home to his family at the end of the day. You know—he helps his wife with the dishes, the kids with their homework, then settles down on the couch to read the newspaper."

"Has it ever occurred to you that someone has to provide him with that news?"

"Of course. The journalist is vital, but he's not the one building a tree house for his little boy, or attending his little girl's school program. He's not around to take her for ice cream so she can show him off to all her friends who are there with their daddies."

"You sound like you're in the market for a father, not a husband."

She winced. "I'd like to think a man can fill both roles. Somehow I can't picture you doing either when you're maybe thousands of miles away researching a story. Though he didn't leave the country, my father was gone most of the time because of business demands. He had the best of intentions, I know, and he provided for me extremely well. But I'd have preferred to go without a lot of things in order to spend more time talking with him, going on picnics, working in the garden together."

She was on the verge of revealing her father's identity when Blackie said, "So what you're telling me is that a man in my line of work doesn't stand a chance with you."

"I didn't say that exactly. You're really a lot of fun. That counts for a great deal. And I like your motorcycle," she added lightly. Jenny hadn't ever put it into words before, but everything she'd been telling Blackie had come straight from her heart. How understanding would he be if she told him who she really was right now?

She heard a funny noise escape his lips. "Is that why you're at O'Brien's? Hoping to meet some boring tourist who'll marry you, buy you a tract house and come home dutifully at five every night to eat dinner in front of the TV set while you juggle the children?"

"Maybe." She ignored his gibes. "I can see I've hurt your feelings. I really didn't mean to. But our conversation just proves what I've been saying all along."

He tugged at a silken lock of her hair. His touch felt like a surge of electricity. "If I were to change careers and do something that kept me on the home front, would you take a second look at me?"

"That's a purely hypothetical question."

He sighed loudly. "Jenny, I may make my living in an unconventional way, but I'm a normal male who longs for a woman to take me exactly as I am. I'd like to think I have enough to offer her that she wouldn't mind a life without all the conventional trappings."

"You mean like clothes?" Jenny couldn't refrain from inserting humorously, remembering his comment about uniforms.

He didn't smile. "Exactly. I want a wife who's as wrapped up in me as I am in her. Who needs anything else?"

"Now you're patronizing *me*, Blackie."

"Don't you want a man who loves you for yourself? Exactly as you are?"

The pounding of her heart almost suffocated her. "Of course. I also want him around more often than a few nights out of every month." Jenny had rarely seen her father more than that. "Blackie...there's something I need to tell you."

"What's the matter? Afraid he'll be unfaithful while he's out of sight?"

"It happens," she said in a subdued voice. She accelerated the truck a little more. "Listen, Blackie—"

But he interrupted her, clearly intent on what he was saying. "Believe me, Jenny, no man would ever look at another woman if he had the good fortune to marry you."

"That's very sweet of you to say."

"It isn't sweet at all!" he thundered. "I was paying you a genuine compliment, but it's obvious I have no credibility. Is that why you haven't married long before now, because you're so evasive no man knows where he is with you?"

He'd come closer to the mark than he knew. Until her father's death, she'd purposely dated wealthy self-centered types who needed nothing more from her than a beautiful woman on their arm. Men like that could never capture her heart. And she didn't dare get involved with a normal everyday man because she'd never know for sure if he was interested in her or in her father's millions.

Fortunately the lights of the restaurant and then the trailer park came into view so she could change the subject. "Home at last."

"From what I know about you," he said, "I'm betting you're the kind of woman who won't sleep a wink tonight, imagining that some killer is stalking you, waiting just outside your trailer.''

Jenny took a deep breath before reacting. If she'd known what the movie was going to be like, she wouldn't have gone. She'd told Blackie that the villain reminded her of the Jekyll and Hyde character, and however superficial the resemblance, the old movie really did terrify her. It still occasionally gave her nightmares. Blackie knew the film tonight had unsettled her; his comment about stalking killers just proved he had a cruel streak of vengeance in him, and it brought out hers.

''Did you learn enough rubbing backs for members of the CIA to protect me if something horrible were to happen?''

There was a long silence. ''When you can't stand to be alone anymore, slip over to my trailer and I'll teach you all I know about the art of massage. Just to show you I don't hold any hard feelings, I'll leave my door unlocked. Good night, sweetheart.'' He leaned across the seat and kissed the end of her nose, then slipped out of the rental truck.

It was crazy, but when she went into her own trailer, she actually jumped as the door slammed shut. Every sound and shadow made her cringe. She rarely overreacted like this. She hated to admit it, but Blackie appeared to know her better than she knew herself.

As she lay in bed, longing for sleep, she realized she hadn't wanted him to leave her alone, despite their conversation, which had turned into a kind of slinging match. Now she was feeling uneasy and wished she could turn on her light. But she couldn't bear to give him that much satisfaction.

The problem was, she'd never lived in a trailer until she'd come to the desert, and she wasn't completely accustomed to being alone. Obviously Blackie had no such qualms. As a journalist, he lived out of a suitcase and could probably sleep anywhere.

His light was still on. Since he'd be the last person to be spooked by a horror film, he was either reading or writing while she lay under her covers, rigid with fear, imagining the worst. When she heard footsteps on the other side of the trailer, she leapt out of bed like a frightened child. It was ridiculous, but all their talk about psychotic killers had frightened her.

Without stopping to consider the consequences, Jenny threw on her quilted robe, stepped into a pair of thongs and left her trailer in a run. There was something reassuring about hearing the sounds of a Mozart piano concerto coming from his trailer as she reached it. He was obviously a classical music lover.

What irony her running to Blackie, of all people, for help! Before she could lose her courage, she knocked on the door, then cried out when it swung open and she discovered Blackie standing there, dressed in another silly T-shirt and shorts.

"Good evening," he intoned, imitating Bela Lugosi again. "Come into my parlor." He grasped her wrists firmly and drew her up the steps. She went along with him as if hynotized.

"How did you know I'd be over?" she was finally able to whisper, pulling one hand away to sweep the hair out of her eyes.

"Because your behavior—unlike mine—is as predictable as that film we saw tonight. Remember the girl who ran out into the woods and—"

"Don't remind me," she broke in irritatedly.

His grin was wicked. "You may have hated the film, but it was based on normal human behavior and normal human fears. You've just proved it. That's why such a 'dumb' movie, to quote Ms. Jenny O'Brien, makes millions for the producers. People love to see something familiar, even if they mock it."

He sounded like her English Lit professor in college—on the days she'd decided to drop in on the class. Her eyes darted around the interior of his trailer. As far as she could tell, it was exactly like hers, except the decor was salmon and brown instead of blue and green. The music was coming from a portable stereo perched on the kitchen table along with a half-eaten orange, the book he'd taken from her truck and a spiral notebook.

"I've interrupted you. I'm sorry, but I—I got scared."

"Don't worry about it. I've been expecting you. Have a seat." He indicated the built-in couch. "Actually, I decided to catch up on some personal correspondence."

"A friend?"

He grinned. "My mother."

"Did you tell her about the horror film?" she asked as she sat down on the edge of the cushion.

"See for yourself." He tossed her the notebook and it landed squarely in her lap.

She lifted her head and gave him a puzzled look. "Why would you want me to read your letter to her?"

He stood there with his hands on his hips, looking dangerously attractive. "For some reason, which I haven't quite figured out, I get the feeling you don't believe I care about my family."

She bit her lip so she wouldn't smile. "I didn't say that, Blackie. I only meant they must miss you a lot. I know I would if you were my long-lost brother."

He blinked. "If you can picture us as brother and sister, then you have a much better imagination than I have!"

She got to her feet and put the notebook back on the table without reading a word. "I think I'm over the spooks now."

"You're sure?" Despite her own determination to resist him, it pleased Jenny that he didn't seem too happy about her leaving.

"Positive. But to be on the safe side, I'll take back the book you borrowed."

His slow smile got to her. "That's right. 'Chloroform in print' is a surefire remedy for what's been ailing you all night long."

Ignoring his teasing, she reached for it, but he intercepted her and hugged it to his chest.

"Sorry, but I'm right in the middle of *The Memphremagog Massacre* and I was planning to finish it tonight. I thought you had a Ludlum novel in your trailer."

"I do, but I finished it. Is Boyd's book as good as his last one? As far as I'm concerned, he's the best mystery writer there is."

"I'm sure he'd be gratified to hear that. As for his latest thriller, I'd say it depends on personal taste. If you like mysteries about the supernatural that take place inside a monastery, I might recommend it. But not tonight. Not with the state you're in."

"It's your fault," she mumbled, running a slender hand through her tangled red mane.

His smile was treacherous. "In what way?"

"It's your Bela Lugosi accent. He terrified me as a child," she said truthfully.

"I thought Spencer Tracy was the villain."

"Spencer Tracy terrified me as a woman."

"What's the difference?"

"I'm not sure. Dracula was terrifying on the outside all the time. But Dr. Jekyll had Mr. Hyde lurking beneath the surface. You never knew when he would emerge. A lot of husbands are like that after marriage, Blackie."

"So are a lot of wives. I think you're tired. Why don't you lie down here on the couch and go to sleep. I'll wake you in time to go back to your trailer and get ready for work. There are only four hours to go."

"Thanks, but I'll be all right now."

"Coward," he accused her as she left his trailer and hurried back to hers, locking herself inside once more. But ten minutes later she was still edgy. She hadn't yet turned off the light and finally decided to leave it on for the rest of the night. She settled beneath the covers, hoping morning would come quickly.

Another noise that sounded like a knock had her springing out of bed with a racing heart. The knocking grew more persistent. She threw on her robe, then stubbed her toe on her way to the door. "Blackie?"

"No, it's Mr. Hyde," said a voice that sounded so authentic Jenny shivered.

She yanked open the trailer door. "That wasn't funny, Blackie."

He gave her a penitent look. "I'm sorry. I couldn't resist. But when I noticed your light was still on, I decided to bring you something to help you sleep."

"What?"

"Me." He shouldered his way inside, leaving her no choice but to back up. "Don't worry, I don't have any plans except to stretch out on your couch. Now go to bed, Jenny. I'm exhausted." He kissed her forehead and turned out the light.

Inexplicably relieved he'd come, she crawled back into bed while he made himself comfortable on the couch. He'd even provided his own pillow. She muttered her thanks and fell immediately asleep.

CHAPTER FIVE

WHEN HER RADIO alarm went off, she thought she was dreaming. But it continued to blare music until she was forced to sit up and shut it off. The time was six-thirty, and she groaned in dismay.

Blackie had gone. She wondered when he'd returned to his trailer. Neither of them could have had more than four hours sleep in total. Their working day would add torment to agony under the circumstances.

With a sense of déjà vu, Jenny caught sight of Blackie chatting with Sharlene when she walked into the restaurant on the dot of seven. Breakfast was out of the question now, but she could see that Blackie had suffered no ill effects from the previous night. In fact, he looked amazingly alive and vital as he put away an enormous breakfast. Jenny's stomach rumbled as she watched him consume bacon, eggs, waffles and juice while Sharlene looked on in fascination.

Praying it was only hunger pangs she was feeling, Jenny hurried to Tom's office for their weekly planning conference. He greeted her with his usual cheery smile.

"I hear you got in late last night."

Jenny smiled back. "Nothing's sacred around Todd's Trailer Park."

He scratched his ear. "If I don't miss my guess, our resident journalist seems to have a thing for you."

Jenny pretended interest in her nails. "Our resident journalist has a thing for any available female, but a woman would be a fool to take him seriously."

Tom eyed her thoughtfully for a moment. "Not to change the subject, but there's a rumor going around the company that Donny O'Brien's one and only off-spring has infiltrated the company under an assumed name, and that she's out to cause real trouble."

Jenny's throat constricted.

"Someone on the board of directors called me about it late last night. Apparently this daughter has a past history as long as your arm, but you'd never know it by Donny. He worshiped the ground she walked on. Still, I wondered if you'd heard anything about it."

Jenny went slowly hot, then cold. She felt as though the ground would open up under her any second now, and she couldn't have said a word if her life depended on it.

"I've decided there might be some truth to the rumor," Tom continued, "otherwise why would somebody as important as Corbin Blackwell come all the way out here looking for a story about truckers and waitresses? Now it *would* make sense if one of those waitresses just happened to be the heiress to a fortune worth millions. Especially with her past track record . . ."

Tom perched on one corner of his desk. "Has he been nosing around here, asking a lot of questions? You know what I mean."

Jenny blinked. Was that the real reason Blackie had come to the desert? To do an exposé of the infamous Jennifer O'Brien? She felt sick to her stomach but Tom didn't seem to notice her distress.

"I didn't think his showing up here was quite as innocent as he led us to believe, but then he didn't get to his place in the newspaper world writing movie critiques. Still, if Donny's daughter is involved in this in some way, then I'm worried. Donny was about the best friend I ever had."

At this point, Jenny could no longer hold back the tears.

"He let me manage this O'Brien's out in the desert because he knew I had asthma and couldn't work anywhere else. I idolized the man, and no matter what his daughter used to get up to, I'd hate to see the O'Brien name dragged out for the gossipmongers. I literally owe Donny my life, and I care enough to see that his daughter doesn't come to any harm. Do you know what I mean, *Jennifer O'Brien?*"

Dumbfounded, Jenny stared at him with huge wet gray eyes. "How long have you known?" she asked in a haunted whisper.

He leaned forward and patted her head. "A couple of weeks now. You looked familiar when you came in for the interview. But the beautiful woman seeking a managerial trainee's job didn't bear much resemblance to the chubby little girl with braces I once met years ago. Still, certain mannerisms, certain ways you said things reminded me so much of Donny I began to suspect you were his daughter. To make sure, I called Vi and she told me the truth."

"I would have told you who I was, Tom," she blurted in a panic. "I just wanted to prove to you that I wasn't as a-awful..." Her lips trembled and she couldn't go on.

Suddenly she was caught in a bear hug and felt rather than heard him chuckling. "I know you would have. Vi told me you sent her a letter and said you couldn't pretend any longer because you were too fond of me. Is that true, Jenny?"

"Yes," she admitted between sobs.

"Well, I have news for you, kiddo. The feeling's mutual. Donny would be over the moon, as he used to say, if he could see the way you've taken to the job so far. I'm proud of you and I'm rooting for you all the way. But I think for the time being we'll go on keeping your identity a secret."

Jenny slowly pulled out of his arms and wiped her eyes with her hands. "Then you're not angry with me?"

He shook his head soberly. "For trying to uphold your end of O'Brien's? Are you daft, girl? Do you think I don't know what your life must have been like, losing your mama when you were a baby? Having to put up with housekeepers while your dad was working more and more hours to deal with his grief? He was a business genius, Jenny, and a fine gentleman, too. But he loved your mother so deeply he never pulled out of it and didn't realize what his unhappiness was doing to you.

"Vi hoped he'd propose to her, but he never did. More than once Marva and I worried about what would happen to you after he died. You'll never know how pleased we were to discover you'd come to train under me. That took guts, Jenny. Real guts. You're Donny's daughter all right... but you're a sight better-looking!''

"Oh, Tom!" She broke down again and ran back into his outstretched arms. "Thank you."

"There's a lot of people who genuinely care about you. Vi, for one. She's never pressed me to give anyone a chance before."

His comment made Jenny laugh, but it came out as a hiccup. "She's always been wonderful to me."

He held her at arm's length. "That's because she saw through to your heart. It's pure gold, Jenny. Just as Donny said it was."

Hot tears trickled down her face. "I don't know what to say."

"Just don't quit on me now. You're learning fast and by the time I'm through with you, you can walk into that board of directors' meeting this time next year and wow them with your O'Brien business acumen. It'll wipe out any rumors about the past antics of a young lady who needed more from her father than he could give. What do you say?"

"I don't deserve you, Tom, but I swear I'll never let you down if I can help it."

"I know that." He kissed her forehead. "Now, what about Blackie? Do you think he's snooping around for a story?"

Jenny averted her face and fought to control her voice. "I have no idea."

"You've spent a lot of time with him already. Has he been asking a lot of personal questions?"

"Some," she admitted, "but they seemed to come up in the natural course of conversation."

"That's exactly how he elicits his information, don't you see?"

"I suppose so." Her voice trailed off as her heart grew heavier. "Are you sorry I hired him?"

"Heavens, no! Particularly since we don't know for sure he wasn't telling us the truth. But if it turns out he's trying to do an exclusive story on you and your dad, I'll have a lawsuit slapped on him so fast he won't know what hit him. His credibility will be destroyed. With your money, you'd be able to hire the best lawyer in the country. That would be death to a journalist."

Jenny shivered at the sudden grimness in Tom's voice. She'd never heard him talk that way before and realized for the first time that he had a toughness people rarely saw. In some respects, he reminded Jenny of her father; for one thing, he was just as protective. He'd be Blackie's match if it came to a showdown, she realized, and wondered why the thought gave her no comfort.

Because you're falling in love with him, a little voice said. *You want him to be the man you've been waiting for all your life!*

"I—I think I'd better get back to the kitchen and check on his progress. To his credit, he's a much better worker than Ron."

"I noticed." Tom smiled. "Marva says Blackie's the kind of man a woman's dreams are made of. Is that true?" He winked.

"Trust your wife on this one, Tom. She knows what she's talking about."

"Then a word to the wise wouldn't go amiss, would it?" Now he was playing the heavy father, but she loved him for it.

"I hear you, Tom. In the meantime, I've phoned several applicants who'd applied earlier for the dishwashing position and one of them will be in next week for an interview. Blackie was vague about how long he needed work, but at some point I'll ask him for a definite quitting date."

"Good idea. I'm impressed that you've thought this out and that you've even got a contingency plan."

Again Jenny experienced that devastating sense of loss. She knew that one day soon there'd be no more Blackie around to drive her crazy and exhilarate her all in the same breath. A Blackie whose motives she couldn't quite trust . . .

"I'll take care of it. Tom—" she gave him one more hug "—thank you for being such a wonderful friend."

"It isn't hard, Jenny. I loved your dad. It's easy loving you. Have a good day, now—and keep your eyes open."

She didn't need the advice, since his questions had already planted a seed of doubt in her mind. But in all fairness, Tom wasn't accusing Blackie. He was simply watching out for Jenny's interests.

Now that Tom and Marva knew the truth, Jenny went back to the kitchen with more confidence. She no longer felt the burden of guilt that had weighed her from the moment she'd applied for the job. Being open with Tom gave her a sense of rightness and belonging she'd never experienced before. She began to believe it was possible to make a success of her life.

Blackie's blue eyes swerved to hers the second she stepped into the kitchen. She wasn't about to let him sabotage her efforts at this stage—if indeed he *was* out to expose her. Did he mean to portray her as daddy's little rich girl who'd grown so bored she'd decided to stir up trouble by playing at a job?

He smiled at her in greeting, his hands never slowing as he dealt with the endless piles of dirty dishes headed for the dishwasher.

"What happened to you this morning?" Blackie growled softly. "I ordered your breakfast along with mine, but you never showed up."

"I overslept." She wasn't about to let him know she'd been in a conference with Tom.

"I'll cover for you if you want to grab a bite to eat right now. Sharlene said she'd get you something fast."

"That's nice of you both, but I'm not hungry."

Jenny could feel his eyes on her as he moved around to her side of the belt. Was he comparing the way she looked now with photographs he'd seen of her in the newspapers? "Now I know what you're like in the morning when you haven't had enough sleep. Maybe it'll perk you up to hear I've planned a party in my trailer tonight. Sharlene's going to pass the word to everyone who's off duty."

"That's a good idea, Blackie. It'll give you a chance to mingle with the others—for your research." She infused her words with as much enthusiasm as she could, but to her dismay, she'd felt a brief twinge of something unpleasant. Under no circumstances did she wish to analyze why the mention of another woman's name should bother her.

His eyes were shuttered. "Last night was too hard on me, Jenny, so I decided to take your advice and go slow and easy." She blinked at this admission. "For tonight, anyway."

Heat suffused her face and neck with alarming swiftness. He'd detected the flash of disappointment in her eyes. Blackie Archer—no, Corbin Blackwell—was too clever by far!

Jenny kept busier than usual for the rest of the day so that she wouldn't think about Blackie and his real reasons for working at O'Brien's. There was less and less doubt in her mind that he was here to write a story about her. If he had his way they'd be together all the time. And she knew why!

In fact, the second he was off duty, he came to the dining room to remind her of his party. His intelligent eyes took swift inventory of her face and figure while she explained that she'd promised to go to Baker with Ann, one of the waitresses. She derived a certain perverse pleasure watching the smile fade from his lips.

"How long do you think you'll be?" He regarded her steadily as she continued to sort silverware at the station.

"I'm not sure."

"I'll wait up for you."

"You don't have to do that."

"That's beside the point, Jenny. I want to be with you." He sounded so earnest. But that was the problem. Blackie always seemed to be there, appraising her with his eyes and sending her silent messages. Messages that said he could hardly wait until they were alone. The worst of it was she wanted to be with him, too.

"I'm sorry. Not tonight."

"Why don't you wait until tomorrow night? Then we can go together."

She averted her eyes, well aware that he wasn't pleased with her plans. "Ann has to go home and wanted me to drive with her. She hates being alone on the highway. I'll tell you what. If we get back before your party's over, Ann and I'll pop in."

Her offer didn't mollify him, and for once she saw a crack in the veneer. She'd tried to behave normally but he could probably sense her withdrawal. Maybe he was afraid she'd caught on to him.

"Has Tom warned you off me?" His astute question was so unexpected she gasped softly. He *was* afraid!

"What are you talking about?"

A tiny nerve hammered at the corner of his jaw. "The other night Tom came off more like a bodyguard than a boss. Is there an unwritten law that forbids me to see you on a personal basis, after hours?"

Her eyes dilated. Had Tom appeared that way to Blackie? She hadn't noticed because she'd been too mesmerized by the conversation and by Blackie's physical appeal.

"Of course not."

"That's good, because he has no conception of how it is between you and me."

Jenny couldn't help but wonder what it would be like to hear that kind of confession from Blackie if he really meant it. "I think you are imagining things, Blackie."

"If he won't give us the same days off, then we'll know the truth, won't we? Be warned, Jenny, I'm planning to spend them with you," he said near her ear before he disappeared from the dining room.

Though she knew exactly why he wanted to be alone with her, the longing to spend time with him, away from the others, had grown into a permanent ache. His husky tone had sounded so sincere she could hardly bear it. Everything was starting to backfire, she thought in sudden panic.

The minute Jenny was off duty, she went out to Ann's car and they left immediately for Baker, a hamlet in the desert en route to Las Vegas.

Ann was a year younger than Jenny and engaged to a man named Brad, who was serving in the navy. Her mom had phoned to say there was a letter waiting for her. Ann was too excited to wait another day for the mail to be forwarded, so she'd talked Jenny into driving home with her.

Ann's mom had a home-cooked meal ready and insisted Jenny eat with them. Jenny had enjoyed their hospitality once before. She'd immediately warmed to the older woman's generosity and friendliness. The visit was a nice respite and gave Jenny a chance to put the situation with Blackie in perspective.

If he was out to expose her, and she was ninety-nine percent certain he was, then she'd make sure she gave him nothing interesting to write about. If he was simply looking for a short-term affair, then she'd already made it plain she wasn't interested. The best strategy was to continue to be a casual friend, nothing more. He'd hate that!

On the way back to the trailer court, Ann went into ecstatic detail about her forthcoming wedding to Brad. Jenny envied her as she quietly listened and made appropriate comments. Other people were able to enjoy an ordinary uncomplicated love affair, but it seemed Jenny was destined for other things. Maybe she'd end up alone like her father, driven to work all hours of the day and night to bury her unfulfilled dreams.

It was after midnight when they got back to the trailer court. Jenny thanked Ann and said good-night before walking the short distance to her own trailer.

"Hi," Blackie called to her out of the semidarkness. He'd been lounging against the side of her trailer with one ankle crossed over the other and his arms folded across his broad chest. The lights from the court revealed he was wearing a polo shirt and shorts. No man had the right to look as good as he did in shorts, or anything else for that matter.

"Hi, yourself. What happened to your party?"

"Did you meet anyone interesting in Baker?" He ignored her question, strolling toward her with a predatory gleam in his eye. "I noticed a couple of truckers coming on to you today."

He couldn't be jealous! "I had dinner with Ann's family," she responded in even tones. "Do you want to come in for a drink and tell me how things went?" Her suggestion was rhetorical, since he'd already started to follow her into the trailer.

She'd no sooner put her purse on the counter than she felt his hands grasp her shoulders from behind. "Are you being provocative on purpose, or do you just naturally drive every man wild?"

Her eyes widened in surprise as she turned around. His hands held her upper arms in a firm grip. The light she'd left on in the trailer threw his chiseled features into stark relief.

"Blackie?" She tried humoring him. "Did you bite off more than you could chew with the women outnumbering the men? I happen to know that Sue—"

But the rest of her comment was lost as his head lowered to hers. His arms went around her, lifting her off the floor so she was molded to his hard body. Her feet dangled helplessly as his mouth began doing the most marvelous things to hers.

Without conscious thought, she slid her hands into his dark hair and gave in momentarily to the hunger that had been building inside her. Maybe it was because she knew he could be an enemy that she felt this incredible excitement. The taste of his lips intoxicated her and one kiss wasn't enough. She began to lose count as she explored the lines and angles of his face, the texture of his skin. His mouth chased and captured hers time and time again until she wanted to become a part of him.

She had no idea how long he held her crushed against his chest. But when she realized that he might never stop this assault on her senses—and that she never wanted him to stop—sanity returned. She tore her mouth from his, suddenly appalled at her abandoned behavior.

"Please put me down," she begged in a breathless whisper.

He continued to hold her off the floor. His eyes were like fiery blue lasers that burned wherever they alighted. "What if I don't want to?" he answered thickly. "You're a flame-haired witch who can move me to tears with your sweetness in one breath, and drive me wild with desire in the next." A nerve throbbed madly at the corner of his jaw. "Who are you? What are you?" He shook her gently.

"Blackie," she cried out in panic, because she wanted answers to the same questions. But this was only a momentary aberration on his part, while she'd responded to feelings deep inside her. Feelings that were growing despite all logic.

Eyes narrowed, he finally allowed her feet to touch the floor, but he kept one hand entwined in her hair. "I love the way you say my name. I love the way you smell and feel and move. I love your hair and eyes, your flawless skin that feels like satin to the touch. You scare the hell out of me."

The next instant he was gone and moments later she heard him take off on his motorcycle. Right now she wished that she, too, could race across the desert floor with the hot wind in her face to try to blot out the memory of his kisses.

That was the risk of playing with fire. You inevitably got scorched. Even Blackie had come close, but he was too clever to be wholly consumed, because his heart wasn't involved. And because he hadn't yet completed his mission.

Jenny envied his control. If he'd decided he really wanted her, she could never have resisted him. That was what was killing her now, the knowledge that a part of her would willingly have submitted. He said *he* was scared, but he didn't know the meaning of the word.

CHAPTER SIX

THE ONLY rational thing for Jenny to do was keep her distance from Blackie until she could leave for Santa Barbara on her next break, which wouldn't be for another couple of weeks.

At this point she didn't think Blackie was faking his physical response to her. Even if everything else was a sham, the chemistry was real—and therefore dangerous. He must have come to the same conclusion, because he didn't knock on her door after returning from his ride in the desert.

For the next few weeks he monopolized her time at breakfast and lunch. But they were rarely alone in the evenings, because his party had had a domino effect, and everyone off duty began entertaining. Mostly they played cards and danced to tapes.

When Blackie did have free time, he was in his trailer writing. To Jenny's surprise he seemed to have reverted to the "slow and easy" plan, a decision that threw her off balance.

His light was on far into the night. She assumed he was doing double duty—drafting future pieces for his weekly columns, as well as working on his research. While he was occupied with his own work she lay in bed every night poring over company ledgers and memos. And after that, she read the first few pages of the same novel over and over again until she finally gave up in disgust and switched off her light.

When her two-day holiday finally arrived, she felt like a prisoner on the verge of being set free. Blackie hadn't said a word about accompanying her, which showed he probably wasn't that interested in her, after all. It was just as well, because she didn't dare spend time with him away from their work, away from the protection of the others.

She set her alarm to go off well before dawn so she could sneak away while Blackie was still asleep. After dressing in shorts and a sleeveless blouse, she slipped into her sandals, locked the door and hurried out to the truck.

Her eyes made an automatic last-minute inspection of Blackie's trailer and motorcycle. All was dark and quiet as she climbed into her dad's truck, which had been delivered midweek looking like new again. She prayed Blackie was too tired to be bothered by the noise and drove slowly down the track to the highway.

An hour and a half later, she could see the huge pink sun rising above the horizon as she went over Cajon Pass outside San Bernardino. It was a typical Southern California morning. A heavy haze hung over everything, but the sun would burn it off within the next couple of hours.

She felt a sharp pain when she realized her father wouldn't be home to greet her. Right now she'd give anything to be able to fling herself into his comforting arms and cry her heart out. One tear, then another, trickled down her cheeks.

If only she could talk to him about Blackie. But even as she was thinking about her situation, she groaned in disgust. If her dad were still alive, she would never have gone out to the desert, would never even have met Blackie. She was shocked to discover that the thought gave her a bleak hollow feeling, totally different from the grief she felt at her father's death, but distressing in its own way.

Deep in thought, she drove for another hour until she could no longer ignore her hunger pangs. A pancake house near the freeway caught her eye and she exited at San Fernando.

The competition didn't look that great, she mused, walking out of the rest room after freshening up. Though she'd only been working seven weeks, she saw the inner workings of a restaurant quite differently now.

For one thing, the busboys looked sloppy as they pushed their carts around, noisily loading dishes. Jenny was revolted by the sight of food being scraped into stainless-steel bins within the customers' view. She praised Tom for insisting that no carts be used. It meant the busboy made many more trips to the kitchen with dirty dishes, but the diner was allowed to eat in peace with no unsightly scenes to spoil the appetite. As a result, Tom paid his help better than average wages for the effort.

All this and more she observed as she made her way to the counter, where there was less chance of having to observe the busboys at work.

The waitresses covering the counter were too engrossed in private conversation to be worried about the customers. She contrasted their behavior with that of

Sharlene and Ann, who made every patron feel important and had something cheerful to contribute no matter the hour.

"May I join you? Say yes, so we can end this cold war." The familiar male voice seemed to come out of nowhere.

"Where did you come from?" Jenny gasped softly. "I didn't see you behind me on the way in." Blackie's unexpected presence shouldn't have thrilled her, but it did.

He slid his hand to the back of her waist, sending an immediate sensation of delight through her body. He looked relaxed and happy, less intense than usual.

His mysterious smile spoke for itself. "I was right behind you. Literally."

She blinked. "You mean you were hiding in the back of my truck the whole way?"

"Under the tarp," he added in a quiet voice. "I was afraid that after the other night, you'd have second thoughts about letting me come with you. So I took matters into my own hands. If you decide to leave me here, I'll have to hitchhike back to Tom's."

"How did you arrange for time off?" she asked haltingly.

"Ron traded time with me and got someone else to cover for him. In return, I'm helping him with a political-science paper for his night class."

Blackie was frighteningly resourceful. "You're very sure of me, aren't you?" She tried not to reveal any emotion.

His body tautened and she saw something flicker in his eyes. "The only thing I'm certain of is the way we both react when we get tangled in each other's arms. The feeling's indescribable.''

She swallowed hard and looked away. That was one point she couldn't argue.

"I should never have kissed you the other night," he whispered. "I haven't been the same since. It seemed best to stay away from you, but when I thought of you gone two whole days, I got homesick for you and made the decision to tag along, come what may.''

This latest stunt convinced her Tom's hunch was correct. Blackie was out to do a story on her! If she weren't so devastated by the realization, she'd admire his resourcefulness. "What will it be?" She managed to smile normally at him. "Blueberry pancakes or strawberry waffles?''

"Nothing for me. I brought a sandwich and ate it a little while ago.''

"Coffee?''

"I have a thermos on the truck.''

She ate her cinnamon toast and drank her milk without saying anything, trying to come to grips with her feelings. Sitting next to him caused her heart to pound sickeningly. She wondered if he had any idea of his effect on her. Finally she gave up the pretense of enjoying her meal and paid the bill. Blackie ushered her out of the restaurant, a supportive hand clasping her elbow, until they reached the truck.

"Don't worry, Blackie, you're not consigned to the back," she said with mock sweetness.

Grinning, he leaned against the door on the driver's side, preventing her from getting in. "How about letting me drive the rest of the way to spell you?''

She might have known. "That's fine with me."

"I'm glad you said that because I really wasn't going to give you a choice."

"Since you saw my accident, I guess you don't trust my driving. I'm surprised you'd dare drive with me this far."

His lips twitched. "I'm a desperate man." Although he meant the comment to be amusing—or did he?—she reminded herself that he was a journalist, a man not easily daunted by rejection.

After helping her into the truck, he went around to the driver's seat and levered himself inside with an economy of movement that underlined his strength and power. As she handed him the keys, he turned to ask, "Where are we going?"

She darted him a covert glance, wishing he didn't look so ruggedly virile in his hip-hugging jeans and faded blue shirt. The sight of his strong, capable hands, the clean scent of his soap—his very nearness—tantalized her senses.

The time had come to tell him the truth. In a little while they'd be at her home and everything would come out, anyway. She was tired of the secrets between them. More to the point, she suspected he already knew about her. It made no sense to continue the charade. "I'm going home to Santa Barbara."

"I've never been to Santa Barbara."

Jenny rummaged in her purse. "It probably has the most beautiful setting of any city in America." She made a show of putting on fresh lipstick to conceal how badly her hands were shaking. "Follow route 5 to Val Verde, then take 126 through Santa Paula."

"Right." As expertly as he seemed to do everything else, he maneuvered the truck through heavy traffic to the freeway and headed north. If he was surprised she'd decided to bring him to her father's house, he hid it well. They drove in silence until later he said, "We must be near the ocean. I can smell it."

"We're almost there."

He flashed her an unreadable look, but followed her directions without comment once they reached town. She chose the scenic route above the old Spanish Mission. They climbed higher and higher into the hills to reach her estate, which overlooked the crescent beach far below.

A private driveway lined with palm trees wound its way through the lush vegetation. Blackie was forced to brake at the gate below the sprawling pink nineteenth-century hacienda with its adobe walls and red-tile roof.

Jenny never failed to be awed by its magnificence and its beauty. She loved the masses of scarlet bougainvillea dripping over the numerous grillwork balconies and the mountains of lavender wisteria that partially camouflaged the swimming pool off the west wing. The Moorish-style fountain pool in the courtyard was also visible from the cab of the truck. Every inch of its hand-painted tile had been imported from Córdoba, Spain.

She heard Blackie draw in his breath sharply as he stared at the house, its exotic beauty framed by fuchsia, oleander and red passion flowers. Those particular colors should have clashed, but in nature they harmonized perfectly.

Blackie whispered something she didn't quite catch. Then he turned his head and gazed at her for endless moments, before he spoke again. "I've only seen one sight more beautiful than this in my life, and that was you in the desert after sunset."

His words confounded her, probably because she wanted to believe that first night had meant something special to him, too. "It *is* beautiful, isn't it?" she began, determined to steer their conversation firmly away from such a risky area. "My father fell in love with this place as a young man. He purchased it after he'd made his first million." Until now she hadn't felt her wealth was anyone's business, but since Blackie had come for the express purpose of doing an exposé on her, he would already know about Donald O'Brien's millionaire status. At this point no purpose would be served in talking around the subject.

"Sweetheart—" his hand left the steering wheel and slid along the back of the seat to play with a tendril of her hair, which wound itself lovingly around his fingers "—this place is worth a great deal more than that."

He was right, of course.

"Not after the 1925 earthquake. No one would buy the hacienda because of the damage. Dad was able to pick it up for a fraction of its value and restore it."

He turned his dark head away from the grandeur of her house toward the breathtaking vista that stretched to the azure ocean. She could almost hear his brain computing the value of the villa and property. If he'd wanted to find out how much she'd inherited, he was beginning to get an idea.

"And this is all yours." His tone was oddly flat.

"Yes," she said with a sinking heart. "Just give me a minute to find my genie and I'll take you on a tour." After all, this was what he'd wanted. An exclusive. He was going to get it, but the outcome would be quite different than he'd imagined. Grim-faced, she reached for her tote bag, lying on the floor of the cab, and felt for the electronic device that opened the gate.

Blackie was trying hard not to show it, but she could feel his inner tension. Apparently this was even more spectacular than he'd been led to believe. "Do you want some help?" he asked wryly as she continued to rummage through her bag.

"It has to be here someplace." Irritably she emptied the bag's entire contents onto her lap, but it wasn't there. "I have this awful feeling I left it sitting on the table in the trailer, along with my flashlight and sewing kit. How could I have been so stupid?"

"Is there no other way to get in?"

"Unfortunately, no. We'll have to find a phone booth. I'll call the housekeeper and ask her to open the gate from the control panel in the kitchen."

"It doesn't look as if anyone's home."

"One of the Riveras is always here."

"Jenny? Look at me." She turned her head in his direction and encountered surprisingly gentle blue eyes.

"What's the matter, Blackie?"

"You can stop pretending now."

"I beg your pardon?"

"Do you think I give a damn what kind of home you come from? If you'd been born in a slum, it would make no difference to me. Who owns this estate? The truth now," he urged.

Her hands tightened on the strap of her bag. *What kind of game was he playing?* "It was my father's until he died. Now it's mine. I'll be happy to show you inside just as soon as Tina opens the gate. Let's go find a phone."

Blackie made no move to start the truck. "Are you trying to tell me this really is your home?" he demanded incredulously.

She closed her eyes for a moment. "Why do you act so surprised?"

"Because of the things Ron told me."

"What things?" When she'd started working at O'Brien's, she'd fabricated a background based on as much truth as possible without giving anything away.

"That you'd recently lost your father and needed to start a career to support yourself. Everything he told me has been borne out. Though you look lovely in that outfit, I've seen you wear it several times before and I realize you probably don't have an extensive wardrobe." Jenny couldn't believe her ears. "And you never leave the trailer court to shop or party in town.

"In fact you hardly eat anything, which leads me to think you're trying to conserve that way, as well. It's obvious you're trying to save your money and I admire you for it. But it's dangerous to fantasize about a fortune you don't have, Jenny. I know you crave security, but wealth doesn't necessarily ensure it. Believe me, I know what I'm talking about."

If he was referring to the fire that had killed his wife, robbing him of his own emotional security, then she *could* believe it. But he in turn could have no idea how early in life she'd discovered that money was no substitute for love.

The one thing this conversation told her was that Blackie couldn't possibly be out to do a story on her. Jenny was convinced of it. He was too emotional, too intense to be pretending. He honestly believed she was down and out, and he was trying to handle her gently. *He didn't know who she was!* She could have cried with joy. Blackie had no ulterior motives, after all!

Moistening her lips excitedly, she said, "Blackie, there's something I have to tell you, something important you need to know."

"I already know," he answered solemnly, interrupting her before she could explain any further. "Otherwise you wouldn't have carried things this far. Will you tell me something honestly?"

She was puzzled—what did he think he already knew?—but she replied with heartfelt sincerity. "Anything," she said, wanting no secrets between them.

His expression sobered. "Is there no one else you could turn to right now? No other relatives or close friends?"

Ron must have made her out to be desperate! "I have Tom and Marva. Ann. But Blackie, you have to under—"

"I mean from the past," he broke in urgently.

"There's Vi, my father's secretary. Listen, Blackie—"

But she never got the rest of the words out. "Jenny," he said on a frustrated sigh, reaching for her hand and pressing his cheek against it. "Let's get rooms at a hotel in town, get into our bathing suits and spend the day at the beach. Tonight will be soon enough for some serious talk. Right now I don't want to do anything but relax with you, away from O'Brien's, away from all our cares.''

Jenny felt exactly the same way and murmured her assent. He kissed the palm of her hand, then started the truck. The feel of his mouth sent a tremor through her body. When she could find her voice she said, ''There's the Santa Barbara Inn right on the ocean.''

''That sounds perfect.'' He flashed her a look that said he could hardly wait to get her alone.

''Take the scenic route to Cathedral Oaks Road and follow it downtown.''

They were off, and she drew in a deep steadying breath, reasoning that tonight would be soon enough to tell him the truth. To tell him why she was using the name Connelly, why it was so important to her to make a good start at O'Brien's before everyone found out that Donald O'Brien's bad-news daughter had inherited the company.

For the first time in her life, Jenny had proof that a man wanted her for herself, and for no other reason. Despite her fears and Tom's suspicions, Blackie thought she was plain Jenny Connelly. He didn't need her connections or her bank balance. He wanted no favors. Miraculously, he seemed to crave her company as much as she craved his. The realization made her feel a euphoria she'd never experienced before. She wanted to savor this day forever.

They pulled up in front of the hotel's main office and Blackie turned to squeeze her hand. ''I'll go in and see about getting us a couple of rooms. I won't be long.''

He climbed out of the cab and Jenny watched his long graceful strides as he entered the lobby. She tried without success to contain her welling excitement at the prospect of spending the entire day with him. Before long he returned and leaned inside her window. "Our rooms won't be ready till checkout this afternoon. Why don't we use the hotel rest room to change into bathing suits? Then we can buy some food and go out on the beach."

Breathless, Jenny could only nod as he helped her from the cab. One arm around her waist, he escorted her inside the hotel where she quickly changed into a modest kelly-green two-piece suit with a white lace beach coat. When she joined Blackie in the lobby, she noticed he was wearing fashionable fuchsia-pink-and-black swim trunks and another white T-shirt with an absurd slogan. He held a large paper sack from the hotel restaurant.

Even without a tan, he attracted the attention of every female in the lobby. But when she walked toward him, his gaze feasted on her to the exclusion of everyone else. As if on cue, hectic color filled her cheeks.

They left their luggage at the desk and took towels and a carryall for the lunch he'd bought. Blackie threw a strong possessive arm around her shoulders and walked her through the breezeway leading to the beach across the street. Unexpectedly he pulled her inside a covered walkway where there were no people and pressed her against the stucco wall. "I can't wait until we get to the beach to do *this*."

Her heart leapt as he swiftly drew her into his arms and found her trembling mouth. To her amazement, her hunger seemed to match his and without conscious thought she kissed him back, returning kiss for kiss. Right now Blackie was her whole world. She couldn't get enough of him. Her response must have fired Blackie's desire, because she heard his low groan and then he was kissing her with new urgency.

"Someone will see us," she finally gasped, tearing her swollen lips from his. They were both breathing hard, his eyes glazed with a passion that left her shaking.

"You're right. We'd better keep going before I forget all propriety and make love to you in plain sight of everyone."

Jenny felt he'd cast some kind of spell over her. Without speaking, they dropped their things on the sand and waded out into the surf. They spent hours cavorting in the swells, touching, laughing, behaving like deliriously happy children. Much later they went back to the hotel to shower and change clothes before Jenny took Blackie to visit the old Santa Barbara Mission.

It was doubtful either of them got much out of the tour. Blackie managed to find private corners and alcoves, kissing her as often as opportunity allowed. In the early evening, they wandered toward the waterfront, where they had a seafood dinner at a pier-side restaurant. This precious time with Blackie, she thought, would remain in her memory as the most romantic of her life.

They drank champagne while he made love to her with his eyes. They talked about silly things and held hands, oblivious to the people around them. More often than not he kissed her into silence, uncaring of onlookers, and reminded her the night was still young.

The sun sank in a fiery blaze, spreading trails of pink and gold glory in the summer sky as they left the restaurant and strolled slowly along the beach to an isolated stretch of sand and palms.

They stopped there, and Blackie sank down beneath the giant fronds, Jenny a discreet distance away. "Come closer," he entreated, tugging her gently until she rested between his legs, her back to his chest. Together they watched the ocean. The night was magical with the rustling of palms, the smell of salt spray, the silvery brightness of moon and stars. Jenny's heart pounded out of control as he wrapped his strong arms around her and hugged her to him.

She nestled even closer when he brushed her glistening red mane aside and covered her neck with hot moist kisses that turned her body molten. His mouth teased the straps of her sundress until they slid down her arms and gave him access to her scented shoulders.

"Blackie—" she cried out with longing, lost to everything but his touch. Every time he kissed her, she felt herself drowning in pure sensation. With an urgency born of need, she twisted around to find his mouth, but inexplicably he held her at a distance.

In the rapidly fading light, the blue of his eyes deepened to cobalt. "I think maybe you're beginning to ache for me the way I've been aching for you. Our problem is only going to get worse living in and out of each other's pockets. You know that, don't you?"

In an instant Jenny's body went taut. *What was he saying?* That an affair was inevitable—and that it was all he could offer because he'd be leaving soon, pulling out when he'd finished his research? She couldn't take it. Not now. In her panic she made a move to get up, but he gripped her arms and held her in place.

"What's the matter? Why are you looking at me so strangely?" He leaned forward and kissed her with unexpected tenderness. "I want you, Jenny. I want to love you all night long."

Without giving her a chance to respond, his mouth covered hers. She gasped in ecstasy as his kiss claimed indisputable possession. Coherent thought ceased as wave upon wave of desire shook her body. Helplessly she clung to him, surrendering herself to his sensual demands.

For the first time in her life she knew what it was to want a man so much that nothing else mattered. Her body yearned for release, begged for it as she covered his face and neck with kisses.

Suddenly the giggles and crude comments of a group of teenagers walking along the beach reached her ears, and Jenny came abruptly to her senses, drawing away from Blackie in embarrassment. He was much slower to react, his eyes still glazed with the passion they'd shared, the entrancement they'd conjured up.

He said something unintelligible and rose lithely to his feet, pulling her with him. "I should never have started this out here. Come on." They walked the short distance to the hotel.

When they reached the door to her room he gently brushed some sand from her cheek. "I'll give you exactly five minutes to freshen up, then I'll be back." He pressed a hard kiss on her mouth, then let himself into the room next door. Jenny entered her room in a daze.

More than anything in the world she wanted to spend the night with Blackie. But it didn't stop there. She wanted to spend her life with him. However, she was very much afraid this was merely an interlude for him, the kind of thing that happened when he met a desirable, consenting woman while on assignment. Later he'd be able to walk away heart-whole and there'd be no questions asked. No expectations.

But Jenny wasn't made that way. When Blackie knocked on her door a few minutes later and discovered she hadn't showered or changed he said, "I'm moving too fast, aren't I? Go to sleep for what's left of the night, sweetheart. I'll meet you at noon for lunch in the coffee shop." He swooped down and kissed the end of her sunburned nose, then returned quietly to his room.

It wasn't until she heard his door click shut that she realized they hadn't yet had their serious talk. He still believed she was Jenny Connelly.

The rest of the night was an agony of guilt and sleeplessness. Blackie didn't know the whole truth about her, and until he did, she'd never be at peace. Not only that, right now she was tormented by the knowledge that he was sleeping on the other side of the wall. All she had to do was knock on his door and she could be in his arms, in his bed, experiencing the rapture those kisses and caresses on the beach had promised.

Had Blackie sensed her inexperience? Or had he turned away because he knew she wanted so much more than he could possibly give?

She couldn't help suspecting he wouldn't have let her go so easily if he'd known she was the infamous

Jennifer O'Brien. Everyone assumed she was experienced with men. Would Blackie have been any different in that regard? Would he have taken what she'd so willingly offered out there on the beach? Or would Jenny O'Brien's reputation have disgusted him? Would he have looked at her with scorn and contempt?

CHAPTER SEVEN

JENNY WAS still awake when morning came a few hours later. Fear of Blackie's rejection had kept her adrenaline working overtime. Before they met for lunch, she had time to call Tina Rivera and make arrangements to go home for a few hours. There was always a pile of mail to deal with, not to mention the usual household problems that accumulated while she was away.

It was too early to call Vi, but before the day was out, Jenny planned to phone her, too. She needed a friend to confide in.

She dressed quickly and went out to the truck, convinced Blackie was still asleep. Last night they hadn't come in until after one. She'd be back before he had a chance to notice she'd gone.

But in that assumption she was very much mistaken. When she pulled into the parking area a few minutes before noon, she discovered an angry Blackie who'd obviously been waiting for some time. He jerked open the door of her truck before she'd even turned off the ignition. She didn't know him in this mood and dreaded his reaction when she told him the truth about herself.

"I'm not going to try to guess where you've been. What surprises me is that you bothered to come back. What in the hell is going on with you, Jenny?"

She couldn't fathom why he was so upset. "I—I woke up early and decided to do some errands before lunch. I thought you'd still be asleep."

He inhaled deeply. "You don't know very much about the male of the species, do you, Jenny? Otherwise you'd have some idea of the kind of night I endured because of you."

This close, she had a vague idea of what he meant. He stared down at her through shadowed eyes, a brooding quality in his expression. It actually enhanced his dark appeal, and she felt a sudden urge to draw his mouth down to hers.

"If you continue to look at me that way, I might do something right here that would shock you senseless."

Embarrassed that he'd seen the hunger in her eyes, she quickly averted her face and climbed out of the truck, painfully aware that he was taking care not to touch her. They made their way to the hotel, in tense silence.

"They're serving brunch on the patio by the pool. Let's eat out there, shall we?" Without waiting for her consent, he grasped her arm and led her to an umbrella table in a far corner, out of earshot of other diners. His touch was wholly impersonal as he assisted her into a chair and beckoned the waiter to come and take their orders.

Jenny couldn't manage anything more than a glass of juice. Blackie ordered coffee. His usual healthy appetite seemed to be missing.

The heavy silence between them made her more and more uneasy. She didn't know how to begin what needed to be said. Blackie took his time drinking his coffee, pinning her with hard blue eyes that gave no hint of what he was really thinking.

Her chin lifted fractionally. "We weren't in time to visit the botanical gardens yesterday. Shall we go there after we check out?"

"I don't think so. I had something a little different in mind." His voice was harsh.

She swallowed hard. He seemed angry and genuinely upset. Now was not the time to talk about anything as sensitive as her real identity. Maybe he was regretting their interlude, she thought with sudden pain. "Look, Blackie. If you'd like to go back to Tom's, just say so. There's nothing keeping me here and I'd just as soon be working. Things have a tendency to pile up after even one day's absence."

He put down the cup. "Why don't we run the errand I had in mind? Then we'll leave for the desert. Let's go to our rooms and check out, shall we?"

"All right," she agreed, a little wary of his mystifying behavior. He came around to help her from the table and they walked back to their rooms as silent as before. It didn't take long for Blackie to deal with the bill and stow their luggage in the truck.

He didn't reveal his destination as they left the parking area and took the road leading into town. For someone who'd never been here before, he seemed to know exactly where he was going. Within minutes he pulled to a stop in front of a small exclusive jewelry store. Jenny had never shopped there but she knew of its reputation. Someone at the hotel must have told

Blackie where to go if he was interested in purchasing fine jewelry.

The man behind the counter appeared to have been waiting for Blackie, because he smiled in acknowledgment and immediately set a tray of rings on the counter.

"Which stone catches your eye, Jenny?"

Astonished that he'd be asking her opinion on something so intimate and personal, she smoothed a lock of hair from her temple, the better to view Blackie. She knew he wouldn't be asking her advice if this was for another woman. And it certainly couldn't be for her, Jenny. Perhaps he wanted something to send to his mother or his sisters.

"Don't you think the woman receiving a gift like this should be the one making the choice? I'm the wrong person to ask because I don't care for diamonds." To Jenny they were symbolic of the frivolous life she'd once led.

Her eyes had darted repeatedly to an exquisite pearl ring in the case and she pointed to it. "To me, a ring like that has greater beauty because it's quieter, less ostentatious."

Blackie nodded to the jeweler to remove it from the case. "Let's see how it fits," he murmured and slid the lustrous pearl onto the third finger of Jenny's left hand.

It could have been made for her, its fit was so precise. She lifted cloudy gray eyes to him in puzzlement. "This is a lovely ring, Blackie. Any woman would be thrilled to wear it."

His eyes gleamed with satisfaction as he turned to the jeweler. "We'll take it." When the man asked if he wanted the ring gift-wrapped, Blackie shook his head. "We're in a hurry." At that pronouncement the blood pounded loudly in her ears.

The jeweler flashed her a smile, and before she knew what was happening, Blackie had ushered her out of the shop and into the truck, away from curious eyes.

"Blackie, what's going on? I don't understand." She shook her head helplessly.

He half turned in the seat and grasped both her hands, running his thumb lazily over the pearl. "What is there to understand? I love you, Jenny. More than I ever thought it possible to love a woman. I want to marry you."

A rush of such intense joy shivered through her body, that for long moments she couldn't speak. She thought she must be dreaming. But on the heels of that joy came fear, because Blackie didn't know he'd asked the notorious Jenny O'Brien to be his wife. When he found out, would his love be strong enough to understand the reason for her deception and to forgive the mistakes of her past life?

"For the love of heaven, tell me what I want to hear!" His voice shook with emotion.

"You know I love you," she whispered at last. Despite the short time they'd been together, despite everything, she'd lost her heart to him completely.

He made a sound like something between a sigh and a groan. "That's all I wanted to hear," he murmured before he crushed her in his arms and began kissing her as if to draw the very breath from her body. The intensity of his kisses swept along a current so powerful she was spinning out of control.

But Blackie seemed to have more presence of mind than she did. He ended the kiss and pushed her gently but firmly away from him. She moaned her displeasure, which forced a low husky laugh from him.

"You can't get much more certain than this, sweetheart, even if it's only been a few weeks. Under the circumstances, I didn't want us driving back to Tom's without my ring on your finger. I've been watching the way every man in the place has been looking at you, fantasizing about you. I want them to know you're mine."

The possessive note in his voice made her tremble with emotion. He loved a woman he thought had very little in the way of material possessions. She could tell he wanted to love and protect and cherish her, give her everything he thought she'd been missing all her life.

Blackie had fallen in love with her for herself and no other reason. He could have no conception of what this meant to her. *He loved her—Jenny Connelly!* This was the supreme moment of her life.

His love was a gift. An incredible, fantastic gift. He knew nothing of her vast wealth or her seat on O'Brien's board of directors. Nor did he have the vaguest idea of the shameful way she'd behaved in the past. She couldn't imagine his reaction when he did fine out; she did know everything would grow more complicated. Right now, though, she needed to savor the joy of this moment just a little longer.

Very soon she'd find the right way to tell him— about her struggles, about the loneliness that had driven her to run with a crowd of shallow, flattering socialites, people who had more money than integrity. She'd tell him about her need to get her father's attention any way she could and her fears that every man she met wanted her only because of her wealth. Men who were as rich as she was wouldn't have looked at her otherwise—money was a basic qualification for membership in their crowd. Men with less money usually managed to make the real reason for their romantic interest apparent pretty quickly. Somehow she'd make him understand what it meant to know that he, Corbin Blackwell, had chosen a working woman from an obscure little place in the Mojave to be his wife. No one without her kind of money could appreciate how she felt. She in turn planned to make Blackie so happy he'd never regret being married to her, whether she was Jenny Connelly or Jenny O'Brien.

"Everyone at the restaurant will think we're crazy," she finally said in a strangled voice, still reeling from the incredible knowledge that he loved her unconditionally.

"Everyone already knows we're crazy about each other. It's no secret I go a little insane when I've been separated from you for more than a few hours at a time. I can hardly wait to tell Sharlene. She'll be the first one to plan a party." He started the engine and swung out into the traffic, throwing an arm around Jenny's shoulders and, despite her seat belt, pulling her close. "Let's head back."

Jenny murmured her assent and nestled even closer, happier than she'd ever been in her life. She was going home to the desert with the man she loved. It seemed so right.

"Jenny?" he whispered some time later, rousing her from a rosy twilight slumber. "Did you know whenever I'm near you I can hardly keep my hands off you? I've heard love could be like this, but I never believed it till I bumped into this gorgeous redhead a few weeks ago."

It was on the tip of her tongue to tell him the same thing, but his comment made her think of the woman he'd once loved. The woman he'd married—and lost. "Tell me about your wife."

He grasped her hand. "Helen was my girlfriend through junior high and high school. Inevitably we fell into marriage. But she was taken from me three days after the wedding ceremony. We never had the opportunity for adult love to grow and develop. You can't compare that situation to the way I feel about you," he told her gently, "so don't even try."

His explanation dispelled any lingering shadows of doubt.

"WHAT'S THIS I hear about an engagement ring?" Tom's voice greeted Jenny the minute she stepped into the snake museum after work the following evening. Marva had told Jenny Tom wanted to see her while he closed up the place for the night. She didn't have to be a mind reader to know why Tom was anxious for a talk. But she'd been too busy since her return from Santa Barbara to find a time that was convenient for both of them.

"I guess everyone at O'Brien's knows about it by now," she said lightly, wishing she didn't have the uneasy feeling she used to associate with a lecture from her father. She glanced around at the seven large aquariums housing different varieties of snakes found in the Mojave, including a granddaddy rattler. All kinds of pamphlets and posters covered the tables and walls, giving a history of the flora and fauna of the area.

Jenny followed Tom as he secured aquariums and checked that there was adequate water and food for the reptiles. He was unusually quiet, which made her more anxious than ever. Somehow she'd have to make him understand that his fears concerning Blackie were groundless.

Suddenly he looked up and stared at her for a long solemn moment. "Forgive me if I'm speaking out of turn, but since your dad isn't around, I feel somewhat responsible for you. Are you absolutely certain you know what you're doing getting engaged to a man you've known less than a month, particularly when you're not even sure what he's really doing here?"

Jenny had known Tom would ask that question, but she didn't take offense, not when it was obvious he had her best interests at heart. "I admit it happened fast, but when I tell you how this all came about, you'll feel differently."

He scratched the back of his head. "Look, kiddo. Don't get me wrong. I can see why Blackie was swept off his feet. You're one of a kind. But even if he's on the up and up, what worries me is that you're doing this too soon after your dad's death. Marva and I were talking about it earlier tonight. Isn't it possible you're confusing love for Blackie with your own feelings of loss, your own needs?"

"No." Jenny shook her head with conviction. "I had a lot of unfulfilled needs while dad was alive, but I didn't hurry into marriage with the first man who proposed to me, or the second, or even the twentieth." Tom's eyes widened at that revelation. "What I feel for Blackie is entirely separate. Love simply happened. That's all I can tell you."

His eyebrows met in a frown. "I'm not saying this very well. Donny's the one who ought to be standing here giving his daughter advice. I'm probably sticking my neck out where it doesn't belong, but answer me one more question. Did Blackie buy a ring for Jenny Connelly or Jenny O'Brien?"

She paused before answering. "I haven't told him who I am yet." At her admission Tom began to shake his head. "Don't you understand what this means, Tom? He loves me for myself!" She described what had happened in front of her house in Santa Barbara. "He believed what Ron told him about me. In the past I've never been certain if a man was trying to get close to me for *me,* or for what my father could do for him."

"Jenny..." He reached over and tousled her hair. "You and I know why you haven't told him the truth yet and I can understand your reasoning. But look at it from his point of view. You let him put a ring on your finger under false pretenses. And there's something else," he said before Jenny could get in another word.

"You might hate me for saying this, but I'm going to, anyway. Has it occurred to you he's been playing you along, pretending to love you for yourself just so you won't catch on? He's a shrewd journalist. Don't you see? When he talked to Ron and found out the kind of story you'd been telling people, he might have decided to go along with it."

Jenny felt a cold hand clutch her heart as Tom continued to outline a scenario that put a totally different complexion on things. "If he wasn't being sincere with me, then he's the greatest actor alive, Tom." Her voice shook with pain.

He sighed. "He'd have to be, wouldn't he? He's Corbin Blackwell, after all. The inside scoop on you and your daddy would sell millions of newspapers."

Jenny grabbed the edge of the table. "I think I'm going to be sick."

He put a fatherly arm around her shoulders. "I wouldn't hurt you for the world, Jenny. All I want is your happiness. And the truth is, you don't know any more than I do if Blackie's only motive for being out here is to write that story on truckers and waitresses."

Tears rolled down her cheeks as she pressed her head against Tom's shoulder. "You're right."

He patted her head. "I like Blackie myself—you know that. But as painful as it is to face, I've had to wonder if he came already primed with information about Jennifer O'Brien...if he decided to pursue you to get details about your life that aren't public knowledge."

She reached into her pocket for a tissue to wipe her eyes. "Then at least I have the satisfaction of knowing I haven't really told him anything yet."

"I suppose it's possible," Tom muttered, "that he's been lulling you into a false sense of security until, little by little, he gets the prize story of the year. I hate to even think it, but..."

Jenny shuddered. Blackie's name was a household word; he was a powerful man and could turn out to be her most formidable adversary. "Oh, Tom!" she cried in anguish. "This has turned into a nightmare."

"I know." He shook his head, sighing deeply. "Particularly because it's also possible he's seen a wonderful opportunity to marry a woman who will set him up financially for life, and if that's the case, he's proposed to *you* under false pretenses."

Jenny's first instinct was to bolt. In the past she would have refused to listen to another word and stalked out of the room, blocking out her pain by jumping in her Porsche and screeching down the coast highway at a hundred miles an hour.

But that was the old Jenny.

The new one was trying desperately to hang on to her sanity and to react like a mature adult. Which meant that she had to consider what Tom was telling her. His cautious warnings were for her own ultimate good.

"I can see I've pulled the rug out from under you," he sympathized with wise sad eyes. "Jenny, I'm beginning to love you like the daughter Marva and I could never have. And I'm fond of Blackie. There's nothing in the world I'd like better than to know this is a real love match, the kind that lasts forever. Maybe it is and I'm just an interfering old fo—"

"I-it's all right, Tom," Jenny interjected with more calm than she felt. "It needed to be said and someone who really cares about me needed to say it. Maybe someday I'll even thank you for it," she said, forcing a tight smile. "If he came to the Mojave to get an exclusive on me and everything's been an act up to now, then I'll confront him with it. Whatever happens, we'll both know the truth about each other before the night is over.''

Tom sighed with relief and hugged her. "Like I told you before, you're a strong woman. I know it won't be easy, but if marriage to Blackie is your destiny, then it'll be worth the risk of walking through fire. Right?''

His comment sounded strangely prophetic. Jenny nodded and left the museum. Tom's suspicions echoed and reechoed in her brain like a grotesque litany. She couldn't stop thinking about them, wondering what was true and what wasn't.

Why would Blackie want to marry a woman he was out to expose? That didn't make any sense. But if he'd come for the express purpose of getting a front-page news story and then decided it would be more lucrative to marry her, that was another matter.

Jenny groaned in despair, no wanting even to admit the possibility, but the nagging fact that he'd proposed so soon after meeting her began to erode her confidence. Was he really no different from all the other grasping men she'd known? Just more clever, more attractive, more exciting?

Tears ran down her cheeks, blurring her vision as she made her way along the track to her trailer. *Blackie, Blackie,* she cried from her heart. *If you're not a hundred percent genuinely in love with me, then God isn't in His Heaven.*

Jenny expected to discover Blackie on her doorstep, because she was late for their prearranged date. But it was Sharlene who called to her as she went up the walkway, and Jenny quickly wiped her eyes. Sharlene's trailer was on the other side of Blackie's, at the end of the row.

"I want to take another look at that ring, now that I don't have to stand in line."

Jenny laughed gently in spite of her pain and lifted her hand for the other woman's perusal.

"It's beautiful. Some of the others were surprised, but I told them they didn't have eyes in their heads."

Jenny could have hugged her. "Believe me, Sharlene, no one was more surprised than I."

"Ah, go on." The other woman chuckled, shaking her blond head in a familiar gesture. "That man was crazy about you from day one. I know because he ignored every other female in this place, if you know what I mean."

"He likes *you* very much." Jenny knew that without a doubt. Whenever Blackie wasn't with Jenny, or in his trailer writing, he seemed to be with Sharlene.

"Blackie likes to talk shop with me. I swear that man gets me going until I don't know when to stop. He must know everything that goes on in my brain. But liking and loving someone are two different things."

"You're right about that," Jenny said in a quiet aside, wondering what Sharlene would say when she found out she'd been confiding in Corbin Blackwell all this time.

"You know," Sharlene said, "my mother used to use the word 'smitten.' She'd tell me so-and-so was smitten with so-and-so. I never knew what that meant until I started watching you and Blackie together. He's never even looked at another woman since he laid eyes on you. That's *smitten* with a capital *S*."

Again Jenny laughed, but inwardly she felt as though she were dying. Sharlene could have no idea of the precariousness of Jenny's relationship with

Blackie. Tom had forced her to see she'd probably been living a fool's paradise.

"I tell you," Sharlene went on, unaware of Jenny's turmoil, "if a man ever looked at me that way, I'd expire on the spot. I know a couple of gals who'd just as soon poison your root beer." She grinned. "But I think you're one of the nicest people I've met. So's Blackie. You two were made for each for other. Congratulations."

Sharlene was the most honest, genuine person Jenny had ever come across. Everything she said came straight from her heart. "Thank you, Sharlene. You'll never know how much your words mean to me. And I'm sure Blackie feels the same way."

Sharlene's smile widened. "From the way he's been talking to me today, I'd say that man can hardly wait to walk you down the aisle."

Her voice was drowned out by the sound of Blackie's motorcycle. "Speaking of Mr. Dangerous..." She smiled. "See what I mean? The man can't stay away from you."

Jenny's heart always gave a funny little kick when she saw Blackie after even the briefest separation.

"How are my two favorite women?" He remained astride his motorcycle, his shimmering blue gaze encompassing them both.

"If we're both your favorites, how come I'm not wearing a ring like Jenny's got on there?" Sharlene chided, her eyes full of mirth.

"Because I happen to know you wear one around your neck and Jenny's never had one."

"Are you married, Sharlene? Tom never said a word. I've never seen you with your husband."

"That's because my husband's in a nursing home in Barstow. He has Huntington's Chorea. I visit him every chance I can."

"I'm sorry." Jenny didn't know what to say. The other woman kept pretty much to herself after hours and always put on such a happy front that her grief wasn't apparent. In a few short weeks, Blackie had managed to get close to Sharlene in a way few others had. He was an expert.

"Will your husband get better?"

"No. It's terminal. I used to be angry, but not anymore. We had ten years before he starting showing symptoms. You know what I say, enjoy life for the time you have it. Blackie's got the right idea."

As she disappeared into her trailer, Blackie's gaze fell on Jenny. "They don't come any better than Sharlene."

"No. I agree."

"I've been looking all over for you. Where did you go after your shift?"

She swallowed hard. "Tom wanted to see me."

Blackie eyed her seriously. "I don't think he's very happy about our news. He was distinctly chilly with me. Accused me of rushing my fences." He vaulted smoothly from his motorcycle.

"Tom said the same thing to me," she confessed, watching for any sign of guilt on his part—and hating herself for it.

"Tom's as possessive with you as a mother hen. I guess you bring out the protective instinct in men. It's a good thing he has Marva or I'd be more worried about his interest in you."

She couldn't help but analyze everything Blackie was saying and didn't want to admit his responses could be interpreted in several different ways.

Darting Jenny a quizzical glance, he put his arm around her shoulders. "I can see we need to talk, but let's get out of this heat first." They moved inside his trailer. "And I've got to have this before we do anything else." Immediately she was in his arms, her mouth crushed beneath his.

Jenny had been anticipating this moment all day, recognizing how desperately she craved Blackie's kisses. It was a moment all the more poignant because of her fear that tonight's talk could alter the course of their lives.

His hunger for her seemed to deepen even as it was being appeased. "I love you," he whispered on a ragged breath, his eyes glazed with desire. But a knock on the door prevented Jenny from telling him she loved him, too, and he reluctantly put her away from him to answer it.

Jenny could hear Ron's voice raised in greeting, followed by conversation. Then Blackie returned. He went to the refrigerator and handed her a cold root beer while he drank Coke. Ever since he'd found out her preference, he kept them on hand. When he took on a project, he learned every facet of it down to the last tiny detail, she mused with unhappy irony.

He stood braced against the kitchen table watching her, a guarded expression on his face. "What else did Tom say that's made you look so worried? I don't like it."

She perched on the arm of the couch and pulled the hem of her skirt over her knee in a jerky motion.

Blackie's gaze took in the elegance of her long slender legs as she crossed one over the other. "He thinks everything has happened way too soon."

"I agree with him," Blackie replied unexpectedly, "though I don't quite understand why he's so preoccupied with our private lives."

She moistened her lips. "He's a good person, Blackie. I wasn't in the best of shape when he hired me. It was too soon after my father's death. He's simply watching out for my interests."

Could a person feign the compassion she saw in the depths of his eyes?

"That's my responsibility now, Jenny," he said as he tossed his can in the wastebasket. The possessiveness in his voice sent a shiver of mingled excitement and foreboding through her body. "Let's get out of here and go for a ride in the desert. I've got some important things to discuss with you in private. If we stay here, we'll be interrupted."

Blackie was leading up to something. She could sense it and nodded her head in agreement. Depending on what he had to say, she'd know whether or not she needed to tell him the truth about herself.

Some of the employees were milling around as they left the trailer and called to Blackie with suggestions for a game of cards. But in his tactful way, he declined. "We're in love, guys. You know how it is. Another time. Maybe." His words were greeted with friendly laughter and ribbing as he helped Jenny into the truck. Then he started the engine and they drove slowly toward the desert.

By the time Blackie had pulled to a stop at their favorite spot a few miles from the trailer court, night had fallen.

"Come on, Jenny." He urged her out of the truck and walked her around to the tailgate. "Up you go." In one lithe movement he lifted her onto the truck bed, then climbed in behind her. She watched in fascination as he spread the tarp and sat down, holding out his hands to her.

The adoring look on his face had her sinking into his arms. He lay down and pulled her with him so they could gaze up at the heavens.

The stars hung in clusters, like diamonds heaped upon diamonds, shining in all directions, light upon light. "Oh, Blackie!" she cried in wonder, not wanting anything to mar her happiness.

"It's a miracle, isn't it?" He rolled on his side and kissed her with raw passion. "So are you. If I had my way, the honeymoon would start right now."

"I feel the same," Jenny admitted truthfully. "But I have to confess I've always wanted to go someplace... special with my husband to start our life together." She'd had a surfeit of travel to places frequented by the jet set.

"Where's that?"

"I'm afraid you'll laugh if I tell you."

Blackie leaned over, his blue eyes searching hers. "Don't ever be afraid to tell me anything. Where would you like to go for our honeymoon?" He sounded so sincere, so eager to please her, she couldn't believe he had ulterior motives.

"It would be out of the question for a lot of reasons."

"I have enough money saved to take you where you want to go, if that's what you're worried about."

The mention of money caused her stomach to clench.

"It's not so much the money as time."

"Now I'm intrigued." He grinned. "Come on. Out with it."

"It will probably sound silly to you, but when I was about fourteen—an impressionable age—my father's secretary gave me a book called *The Garden of Allah*. I loved it so much I must have read it a hundred times, and—"

"You want to go to the Sahara with me." It was as though he'd read her mind.

"How did you know?"

"I loved that book, too."

"You did?"

"I've been a voracious reader all my life. Shall we hire a caravan and ride off into the desert like Boris and Domini? Lose ourselves in each other for weeks on end in God's garden, away from civilization?"

His gaze seemed to melt her bones. Everything he said and did made her fall in love a little more.

"It's too unrealistic," she whispered, wishing she hadn't said anything, knowing it was wrong to go on fantasizing when everything could blow up in her face any minute.

"Not at all," he murmured. "I found you in the desert. I can think of no more romantic place on earth than the Sahara to make love to my bride. We'll take it slow and easy. No deadlines, no pressures. You're the most important thing in the world to me."

She raised her hands to his face, trying to read the truth behind every word, every look. "I adore you, Blackie. You have no idea how much," she whispered, her voice throbbing.

"I think I do," he said on a ragged breath and buried his face in her glistening red hair. "I never thought I'd find a woman who'd curb my restlessness." The tremor in his voice was so real it led her to believe that despite his exciting career as a journalist, he'd suffered in ways most people would never understand.

"Jenny, I've been thinking everything out." He fingered a silky strand of her hair as he talked. "When we get our next days off, I want you to fly to Vermont with me to see if you'd like it there. Enough to live permanently."

Her stunned expression wasn't lost on Blackie, who traced the curve of her mouth with his finger. "You're a California girl, and from what I've gathered, Californians rarely want to live anywhere else. But I was hoping you'd give Newport a chance."

Jenny sat up, instantly alert and confused. "I thought you worked out of New York."

Blackie raised himself to his elbows. "It's been a base from which to operate, but I've never considered it home. Home is a place where there's someone waiting for you at night, someone who loves you. I haven't known that luxury since my youth."

Again she heard that unmistakable nuance in his voice that told her he'd always craved the really important things in life. Was his acting ability so great, he could *pretend* the raw emotion she heard? "Do you want children?" he asked unexpectedly.

She blinked. "Of course." The thought of a little Blackie and Jenny running around made her heart swell with yearning.

"Right away?" He sounded eager. She couldn't believe it.

"Do you?"

In response he reached for her and kissed her tenderly. "Since I met you, I hunger for roots. With you I'll have a home and a family. Just imagining you pregnant with our child makes me hurt, I want it so badly."

Did he mean it—or was he thinking of her money and how beautifully it would keep them all the days of their lives?

"I know how much you miss your father, and since you have no living relatives, I thought it might ease the pain to be near my family. They'll adore you."

Everything he said tore her apart, because he sounded like a man deeply in love and ready for life's most binding commitment. She bit her lip. "Does your whole family live in Newport?"

"Mom and Sarah live there. Justine's in East Corinth, which isn't that far away."

A trembling started deep inside her body. "I can't imagine anything more wonderful than being married to you and surrounded by your family."

His eyes flickered with satisfaction, yet he seemed hesitant, a reaction totally unlike the Blackie she'd known up to now. "How would you feel about being married to the editor of a small-town newspaper?"

At this point Jenny got to her knees and stared down at Blackie, her arms hugging her chest. "What do you mean?" She never knew what he was going to say next. From prominent journalist to editor of a small-town paper meant a drastic change in focus and life-style. *And salary,* a tiny voice nagged.

Blackie shifted so that his back rested against a side panel of the truck. "Meeting you has changed everything. My days as a roving journalist are over. How can I possibly take you and our children on picnics and build tree houses in the backyard of the beautiful home I have in mind if I'm off researching a story on the other side of the world?"

She gazed at him for an endless moment. "You mean because of me, you'd give up the career that has made your name and your living all these years?" If he was being truthful, then such a sacrifice constituted the greatest proof of his love for her. But Tom would caution her it wasn't entirely a sacrifice; Blackie might be losing his salary, but he'd be gaining an heiress for a wife.

"That's exactly what I mean, Jenny."

She sank back onto her heels, hands clenched at her sides. "You'd really like the idea of just being an editor after everything you've done and accomplished?"

"It's in my blood. My mom and dad ran the *Herald* until he died. But it was always a fight to make ends meet and without Dad, Mother was forced to sell. Until I married, I worked with them gathering news. The whole family got in on the act.

"The point is, the *Herald* has grown and been bought and sold several times since, and right now it's for sale again. I'm thinking of buying it and building the circulation. But only if it's what you want, too. I was hoping you might like to work at it with me."

She bowed her head. Had Blackie been saving and struggling to find a way to get back the family business? Was it a matter of pride? Jenny could understand that well enough, but she also understood the price tag that came with such a transaction. Her heart began to thud sickeningly. "Wouldn't that cost a small fortune? More than you make as a journalist?"

There was a long pause, as if he were troubled and searching for the right words. "A great deal more, and that's what I need to talk to you about."

Suddenly she knew what was coming. It was like the feeling she'd had when she was about to crash and couldn't do anything to prevent it.

CHAPTER EIGHT

"JENNY, there's no easy way for me to say this, but I haven't been completely honest with you concerning certain aspects of my life, particularly my financial situation."

"I know," she whispered, feeling something precious die inside her. "I guess that makes us even, considering I wasn't totally honest with you, either."

His dark head reared back and his body tautened perceptibly. She thought she saw a momentary flash of pain in his eyes. "I swear I didn't mean to hurt you, Jenny. I came out here to do a very special story, a pivotal story, and probably the most important one of my writing career.

"You have to understand a writer is very much like an undercover detective looking for clues without anyone's being aware of it. I needed to be the proverbial fly on the wall, thus the reason for my alias. But there's so much I need to explain. How did you find out?" The starlight revealed his sudden pallor.

"Several weeks ago Tom mentioned his suspicions to me." She couldn't keep her voice from cracking.

Blackie looked astounded. "How did he find out? Why didn't you say something then?"

"I don't know how you can ask me a question like that!" She lifted wet, accusing eyes to him. "I was in love with you, Blackie! I didn't want to believe it."

A look of puzzlement crossed his face. "Sweetheart, you act as if I've done something monstrous. In hindsight, I realize I should have been honest with you from the very beginning, but how was I to know I'd fall in love with you? Nothing could have been further from my mind when I flew out here a month ago."

"That doesn't surprise me. The story was everything. But you should've been more discreet and waited a little longer before showing up on the pretext of needing a job. You overplayed your hand, and that's where you made your mistake with Tom. I was too crazy about you to suspect any hidden motives."

Blackie rubbed the back of his neck in seeming bewilderment. "I think we're talking at cross-purposes. What do you mean I should have waited longer before coming to you for a job? You're not making sense."

"Stop pretending, Blackie. We both know that somehow you found out I was working under cover at O'Brien's and saw the perfect opportunity to do an exposé on me. And why not?" Her voice shook with pain. "I've been fair game to the press for years now. When did you decide to change tactics and marry me, instead?"

His hand reached out to seize her wrist. "What in the hell are you talking about?"

She could hardly focus on his face for the tears. "Are you trying to tell me you don't know I'm the infamous Jennifer O'Brien, daughter of Donald

O'Brien, California's restaurant king? You don't know I'm the principal shareholder in the O'Brien Restaurant chain and heiress to a fortune estimated at twenty million dollars last tax audit?''

His grasp tightened and he stared at her as if he'd never seen her before. ''You told me your name was Jenny Connelly.''

She tried to pull away but her efforts to escape his firm grip seemed to infuriate him. ''I realize being found out must have come as a blow,'' she went on. ''More than ever I understand why my father revered Tom Burch. Nothing gets by him. Nothing and no one, not even the famous Corbin Blackwell!''

''Is that what you really think?'' he hissed.

''I hate to tell you this, Blackie, but you're really no different from any number of men in my past anxious to get their hands on my father's money. But to your credit, buying back the hometown newspaper to honor your father's memory puts what you've done in a slightly different light.''

At those words he let go of her arm as if the touch of her skin had scalded him. An inscrutable mask slipped over his face. It should have warned her something was horribly wrong, but she was in too much pain to prevent herself from retaliating with the only weapon at her disposal.

''How much do you need, Blackie? One million? Two? I have no idea what it costs to buy a newspaper these days, but considering you've gone to such extraordinary lengths, I'll lend you the money. Just have your attorney get in touch with mine at O'Brien's home office in Santa Barbara.''

She pulled the ring off her finger and tossed it at his feet. "You can get a refund on *this* and apply it to the down payment on your newspaper."

By this time, his expression had undergone a total transformation, and the silence stretched endlessly between them. Finally his lips moved, but the voice didn't sound like Blackie's.

"After listening to you, Ms. O'Brien, I can understand why your reputation precedes you." With enviable calm he scooped up the ring, closing his hand around it in a fist. "Lucky for me your true nature asserted itself before I found myself married to the wrong woman."

His eyes held a murderous glint. "I wonder how long you planned to keep your identity a secret. It's not nice to lie, but then everybody knows you're not a nice little girl."

The look of revulsion reflected in his eyes told her more clearly than words that she'd misjudged him completely. Unforgivably. The loud buzzing in her ears warned her she was close to fainting.

"Don't," she whispered, shaking her head, not able to bear his scorn. "Blackie... please. You don't understand. I'm so sorry. Please, hear me out. Forget everything I said and let me start over again. This is all more complicated than you could possibly imagine."

"Don't you mean more sordid?" he lashed out. "Since I was led to believe you were penniless, I couldn't possibly have been after your money. How much did you pay Ron to spread the colossal lie? It's pitiful that you never learned some things in life are infinitely more precious than money."

"I tried to tell you when we drove to my house in Santa Barbara but—"

"But you didn't try hard enough and let me go on believing Ron's version," he interrupted. In a lightning move he jumped down from the back of the truck.

"No, Blackie!" She attempted to defend herself, the tears trickling down her pale cheeks. "It wasn't like that. I just want the chance to explain. I'll tell you everything from the beginning."

"Keep your millions, Ms. O'Brien," he said, ignoring her entreaties. "From all I've heard about you, you'll run through them long before your looks fade. *Then* what will you do? There'll be no more daddy to keep you when you're tired of your little working-girl games."

"Blackie!" she cried to his retreating back. "Don't walk away from me yet. Give me a chance to explain!"

He paused midstride and turned around. "You know, there's only one person in the world more frightening than Mr. Hyde, don't you? It's *Mrs.* Hyde. The only horror film I don't have the stomach for." Then he was gone.

His words twisted like a knife. She listened until she could no longer hear any sound before collapsing on the tarp in a paroxysm of tears. She'd unfairly accused him of something that went against his innate decency, and in the process, she'd lost him. The pain was unendurable. She lay down on the floor of the truck in a stupor.

When the first lavender rays of morning lit the eastern sky, she became aware of her surroundings and realized how much cooler the air had turned. With a little shiver, she staggered off the back of the truck and went around to the cab. Blackie had left the keys in the ignition.

She turned on the engine and started back toward the trailer court, unable to imagine how she'd survive the day. As she pulled to a stop in her parking space, her eyes automatically darted to Blackie's trailer. To her surprise, his motorcycle was still there. Considering his frame of mind, she wouldn't have put it past him to leave without giving notice.

With only an hour to go until she had to report for work, Jenny spent her time in the shower and tried to repair the damage to her ravaged face. She wasn't going to give Blackie the satisfaction of seeing the toll his repudiation of her had taken.

Until he left O'Brien's, and she had no doubt it would be right away, she'd have to put on the greatest performance of her life, not only for him, but for everyone at the restaurant. She'd lost the two men in life she'd ever loved. All that was left was her work. Right now it was her only salvation.

She heard Blackie's motorcycle before she left her trailer and was thankful she hadn't stepped outside at the wrong moment. The thought of having to confront him, or even to look at him, was more than she could bear.

Needing to bolster her badly shaken confidence, she slipped on a cool lace-trimmed dress she'd bought in Mexico. A matching bandeau kept her hair out of her face but left it flowing to her shoulders. The outfit was new but casual enough for work and she needed to look her best if she expected to deal professionally with Blackie.

A few minutes later she walked into the restaurant and headed immediately for her office. Ron and Betty were effusive with their compliments. Jenny could only hope she didn't look too made up. She rarely wore anything more than lipstick and a little blusher.

There was a phone message to say that one of the applicants for the dishwashing job would be arriving for an interview the following day. Under the circumstances, Jenny felt the timing couldn't be better.

Before she started on the payroll, she had to do her morning rounds to ensure that everything was running smoothly. That meant a trip to the kitchen to consult with the chefs and Sharlene, who was the head waitress. She'd have to check on Blackie's progress, too, but the mere thought caused her heart to plunge.

"Well, don't you look like something!" Sharlene's face lit up in a bright smile as Jenny walked through the dining room. "And here I was going to ask you to wait on tables. Ann has a headache so I told her to take an aspirin and go lie down for a while."

"I'm glad she took your advice," Jenny said in a low voice, hiding the ache in her heart with a smile of her own. "I'll cover her area and do the payroll later in the day."

The pert blonde cocked her head to one side. "Are you sure you and Blackie aren't planning on running off to Vegas to get hitched after work? You look fantastic."

"You're good for my ego, Sharlene." She paused. "Blackie noticed that I was wearing the same outfits over and over again, so I thought I'd put on some-

thing different for a change." Jenny didn't plan to say
anything about her broken engagement; if the situation arose, she'd leave any explanations up to Blackie.
With luck, no one would notice the ring was missing.

"You'll knock his socks off. I'd like to see his face
when he gets a look at you." She grinned.

"You're an incurable romantic, Sharlene. Listen,
I'll go back to the kitchen and check things out. Then
I'll start waiting tables. Give me two minutes."

"Thanks, Jenny. Just between you and me, the last
day manager never went out of his way for anybody.
The difference between the two of you is like night and
day. That's what I told Tom."

Tears smarted in Jenny's eyes and she looked away
quickly so Sharlene wouldn't notice. "Thank you,"
she whispered as she headed fearfully toward the
kitchen. The other woman could have no idea how
much Jenny needed to hear those words of praise right
now. It was all that kept her going.

The kitchen was its normal den of organized com-
motion, but her thoughts were so heavily concen-
trated on Blackie she went through her normal tasks
by rote, without really seeing anything. Seconds after
her conversation with the chef, she couldn't even recall what they'd discussed.

Blackie was standing in his usual spot, wearing his
green uniform top over a T-shirt and jeans. The sight
of him, conscientiously performing his job, brought a
fresh wave of pain, but before she could turn away,
their eyes met.

His were a forbidding arctic blue that cut through
her like tiny shards of ice, destroying even the slight-

est glimmer of hope that he'd had a change of heart during the night and was now prepared to listen to her.

Jenny fled the room and began waiting tables, grateful to be swept into the kind of work that didn't allow her body or her mind a moment's respite. The first day she'd come to work for him, Tom had shown her a job survey that rated waitressing as one of the most stressful occupations for women. But right now Jenny welcomed the demands that ran her off her feet and kept her from thinking.

After lunch, a grateful Ann relieved Jenny and promised she'd make up the favor somehow. With Brad, her fiancé, arriving that evening, Ann hadn't slept at all the night before and got up with a splitting headache. Jenny said she understood and assured Ann that they were even after her mom's wonderful home-cooked meals.

The remainder of the day Jenny spent in her office, outside Blackie's orbit. She worked through the dinner hour to finish the payroll and ate a sandwich one of the waitress brought her.

Tom and Marva had taken the day off to go to Barstow, so there'd been no opportunity to tell Tom anything. Jenny wasn't sure she'd survive reliving the experience. The memory of her final exchange with Blackie produced a pain so deep she wondered if it could ever heal.

A little after eight she left the restaurant in a kind of daze, climbed into the pickup and headed for the trailer. After an almost sleepless night and a full day's work, perhaps she'd be able to sleep without thoughts of Blackie tearing her to pieces.

"Jenny?"

At the sound of Blackie's voice, she whirled around in shock. A familiar burst of adrenaline had her heart pounding fiercely. He was standing on the bottom step of his trailer dressed in khaki pants and a white shirt. She thought he'd never looked more handsome and appealing, but she didn't understand why he was even speaking to her at all.

"Yes?" she asked in a dull voice.

"I think you need to know the day crew has planned a party for us tonight. I overheard Sue telling Ron in the kitchen. I was just coming to get you."

Jenny's chest heaved at the news and she shook her head. "I can't."

"We're going to have to show up and pretend all's well. Sharlene's gone to a lot of trouble and expense. We can't disappoint her. It's in her trailer."

"I don't feel that well," she murmured and turned away. But Blackie grabbed her by the shoulder and spun her around, his eyes angry in a face dark with scowling.

"Still living up to your reputation as the selfish little brat who exists only for her own pleasure?" His barb stung, but she'd rather die than let him know he had the power to hurt her anymore.

"You're right. I'm every awful, ugly thing people say I am. But since it's Sharlene, I'll rise to the occasion. Tell her I'll be along in a minute. I need to freshen up first."

Blackie's eyes roved insultingly over her face and body. "Why bother when you know you're more beautiful after thirteen hours of work than any woman has a right to be? Here. You're going to need this tonight."

With barely controlled impatience he grasped her left hand and slid the ring on her finger. His touch sent a shock of awareness through her body and she stepped back, afraid he'd see how much the slight contact affected her.

"I'll wait here," he warned as she turned to enter her trailer. Obviously, he was implying that she'd better not get any ideas about avoiding him or staying away from the party.

Once inside, her hands literally shook as she pulled off the bandeau and ran a brush through her hair. After touching up her makeup and dabbing on some perfume, she went back outside, anxious to get through the ordeal as quickly as possible and go to bed.

Maybe it was her imagination, but she thought Blackie looked at her in the old way when she came out of her trailer. Of course she must have been mistaken, because when he grasped her hand, startling her, the narrowed blue eyes were accusing and remote.

"How soon can you find another dishwasher to replace me?" he asked in a low voice as they walked the short distance to Sharlene's trailer. Music was blaring and people were coming in and out of the trailer with drinks in their hands.

"I'm interviewing a man in the morning."

His hand tightened almost painfully on hers. "I've given my notice, so the sooner you hire someone, the sooner I can leave."

She sucked in her breath. "If his references check out, I'll hire him on the spot."

"Am I supposed to train him?"

Jenny couldn't imagine Blackie wanting to stay around long enough to do that. "Your work is temporary. I'll take care of the training."

"But then, that's part of your job, isn't it?" he taunted.

She lifted her chin defiantly. "Why don't you leave tonight after the party? The restaurant will survive."

"Is that a suggestion or an order?" he asked in scathing tones.

"Take it any way you want. I really don't care."

"Once we're inside, you'd better put a smile on your face or you're going to hurt Sharlene's feelings," he whispered, brushing his lips against her cheek as a couple of employees called out to them.

"Maybe I could do that if you weren't crushing my hand."

As if unaware how tight his grasp had been, Blackie stared at their hands, releasing a little of the pressure. He lifted her hand to kiss the palm, then let it go completely.

The feel of his lips against her skin sent waves of yearning through her body. No matter how cruelly he treated her, Jenny's senses were so finely attuned to his, her reaction was automatic.

Thankful for the break in contact, she entered Sharlene's trailer ahead of Blackie, then shuddered when she felt his hands slide up her hips and grasp her waist with an intimacy everyone noticed.

Jenny tried to move out of his hold but his hands remained firmly in place, giving the impression that they were lovers who couldn't bear to be out of each other's arms even for a second.

With more than a dozen people packed in the small trailer, there weren't enough seats and Jenny was forced to sit on Blackie's lap while they ate corn chips and guacamole. Everyone was drinking margaritas, but Jenny declined.

As for Blackie, he'd always seemed a temperate man, but tonight she watched with growing unease as he downed his third drink and reached for a fourth. Since the night she'd heard about her father's fatal heart attack, Jenny hadn't touched liquor. She'd never really liked it, anyway, and wasn't drunk nearly as often as the gossip columnists had intimated. Being the life of the party had been an act. No one—not her so-called friends, not the press—had known of her inner agony, her struggle. Now she associated alcohol with the emptiness of her former life and had given it up.

As the crowd grew noisier and the music more raucous, she recognized the glazed expression in Blackie's eyes, the only noticeable sign that the amount of alcohol he'd consumed was affecting him.

Blackie's dark head bent closer to hers, as if he were whispering something loverlike for her ears alone. "If you're trying to prove you've changed your public image by not getting plastered, let me assure you I'm not impressed."

"Please don't say anymore, Blackie," she begged, but he was too intent on punishing her to pay any heed.

"You and I both know the real Jenny O'Brien still lurks beneath this gorgeous facade, don't we? No alcohol on the job seems to have done wonders for you. Maybe that's why I didn't recognize you in the flesh.

Tell me something. Were you always hung over when your photograph was taken? Did you even know it was being taken, or were you too wrapped up with your latest lover to notice?'' he taunted.

Her retort never made it past her lips because Blackie's mouth descended. To her humiliation, he began to kiss her in plain sight of everyone. She was helpless in his powerful arms, yet fighting him would raise eyebrows, to say the least.

''Your image with everyone at O'Brien's is going to suffer if you keep this up,'' Jenny whispered when he finally allowed her breath. ''I don't think Sharlene intended us to bring the bedroom into her living room. She's a wonderful decent human being and I have no desire to offend her.''

He stared at her through half-closed lids. ''From what I've heard, you never used to worry about little things like that,'' he baited unmercifully.

Jenny swallowed her anger. ''Daddy's death turned my world upside down,'' she admitted in a hoarse whisper, but she had no opportunity to explain further because Sharlene started tapping on her glass, asking for everyone's attention.

''As you all know, we're celebrating Blackie and Jenny's engagement tonight. Okay, you two, we have a little present for you to hang in your home after you're married. Come on over here and open it.'' She beckoned to Jenny who with a profound sense of relief escaped Blackie's arms.

Her legs almost buckled as she walked through the assembled group to the kitchen counter, where Sharlene gave her a warm hug.

"Since we know how much you two love the desert—because that's where you sneak off to every night," Sharlene said in an aside that had everyone hooting and hollering and, on cue, turned Jenny's face scarlet, "Ron volunteered to drive out to your favorite spot and take a picture. Then we had a local artist paint it so that fifty years from now, you'll remember how it all happened right here at O'Brien's in the Mojave."

With trembling hands, Jenny unwrapped the present. At that moment, she couldn't have looked at Blackie if her life had depended on it.

The scene staring back at her was the very place where Jenny had known such joy and despair with Blackie. The picture caught the colors of the evening sky, reminding her forcefully of the first night Blackie had kissed her. She could hardly talk for the lump in her throat.

"I—I'm sure I speak for Blackie when I say that I've received many gifts in my life, but never one that has touched me as deeply as this. Thank you," she said to Sharlene alone, then turned to the others. "Thank you, more than you'll ever know." As she looked around the group, she realized that these people were truly her friends.

"Jenny's right," Blackie said in his low, rich voice. He sounded as moved as she did. "Nothing's ever meant more. The Mojave is full of magic and enchantment, but I would never have discovered that if it hadn't been for all of you at O'Brien's making me feel part of the family. I wish there was a better word than thank-you."

While everyone cheered, someone asked, "Have you two set a date?"

Feeling distinctly light-headed from too much emotion, too much pain, Jenny couldn't see to form the necessary words. She avoided Blackie's eyes, leaving the answer up to him.

"As you all know, my job is temporary, and as soon as Jenny hires a permanent dishwasher to replace me, I'll be going back East to another job that's waiting for me. Since her work is here, we've got a lot to sort out before we make final plans. But in the meantime, I'll ask her to keep our beautiful painting in her trailer."

His smooth delivery washed over the crowd and everyone seemed perfectly satisfied with his explanation as they went on partying. Except for Sharlene, whose keen gaze roved from Blackie to Jenny and back again.

Unable to bear her inquiring glance, Jenny started to rewrap the painting to protect it. Blackie made his way to Sharlene's side and kissed her warmly on the cheek, expressing his appreciation.

"One day you'll know the depth of my gratitude for all you've done for me, Sharlene."

"Ah, go on," she said, but Jenny saw the affection the older woman felt for Blackie.

He placed one hand around Jenny's waist and, with the other, relieved her of the painting. "I think we'll slip away while we can still maneuver." He smiled broadly at Sharlene, and Jenny's heart seemed to turn over. More than anything, she wished he were smiling at *her* like that.

"What did I tell you?" Sharlene turned to Jenny. "He's Mr. Dangerous with a capital *D,* and getting more dangerous all the time. You'd better hogtie him quick. I'd hate to see him let loose with all those East Coast women just dying to get their hands on a real man."

Jenny heard Blackie's low chuckle as she attempted to recover from the implicit warning in the other woman's words. If Sharlene only knew the half of it, Jenny groaned inwardly.

"Sharlene, you have the amazing ability to make a guy feel important. Stan's a lucky man. Thanks again." He kissed her cheek once more, then ushered a shaken Jenny through the crowd, which was growing more mellow by the minute.

As soon as he'd guided her outside into the hot desert air, Jenny tried to pull away from his grasp. He wouldn't let her go. "There's no need to accompany me any further, Blackie," she whispered angrily.

"There's every need. Otherwise our other friends—" he nodded toward the group lounging on the trailer steps "—will grow as suspicious as Sharlene. When I follow you inside, as I'm expected to do, let's not have one of your famous O'Brien tantrums."

CHAPTER NINE

JENNY ALWAYS LEFT one lamp burning in her trailer so that she'd never have to enter it in total darkness. She watched Blackie carefully lay their painting on the table and then turn to her, a strange glittering look in his eyes.

"You can go back to your trailer now," she told him quickly. "No one will notice."

He made no move to leave. "You sound as if you'd like to get rid of me, sweetheart, but I have news for you. I'm not going anywhere." As he closed the distance between them, she backed away in panic.

Blackie's mouth twisted. "Fool that I am for not recognizing you from day one, I took it too slow and easy in Santa Barbara. But before I leave the Mojave, shouldn't I have a chance to sample what so many other men have already enjoyed? With the kind of reputation that's been your trademark, it ought to be a night to remember."

"No, Blackie," she begged, but before she knew what was happening, he'd crushed her in his arms and was covering her mouth with smothering force, demanding a response. There was no loving, no caressing, no gentle persuasion.

"Stop! Blackie, please!" she cried as he picked her up in his arms and started for the bedroom. "I've never been with a man before!"

His mouth lifted from hers long enough to hiss, "What lies are you telling me now?"

Breathlessly she said, "I've never gone to bed with a man. Despite everything you may have heard about me, that's the truth!"

His eyes narrowed. "I almost bought that once, but you're no longer Jenny Connelly!"

Suddenly the fight went out of her. "With all the bad press that's followed me over the years, I realize there's no way to convince you. And . . . and I realize you won't forgive me. All I can do is hope you'll go . . . because you once loved me. I don't want it to be like this between us. I just want you to go." Her voice broke on the last words.

At first she thought she hadn't got through to him, because a lock of her glistening red hair was still caught in his fingers. Jenny closed her eyes and turned her head away in defeat.

"Jenny," Blackie said, his voice hoarse. "I'm—"

A knock sounded at the door. Blackie let out a curse and unexpectedly lowered her to the couch. He stood there with his hands clenched, breathing heavily, staring down at her as if he'd never seen her before.

"Jenny? Are you awake? It's Ann."

Jenny smoothed the hair away from her forehead and got up from the couch, but the room was spinning. Blackie stood there unmoving, his eyes fixed on her face. "Just a minute, Ann." She somehow managed to keep her voice from trembling.

"Oh, good. You're still up. Listen. Brad's over at my trailer. We just drove in from Baker. He wants to meet you and Blackie, but we were too late for the party. Why don't you come over for a little while and bring Blackie with you?"

"I—I'll have to find out if Blackie's still awake, but you can count on me. I'll change and be right there."

"Great. I told him you're going to be my maid of honor. We're trying to finalize our wedding plans. See you soon."

As Ann's footsteps receded, an ominous quiet pervaded the trailer. Jenny clasped her hands together despairingly. "I think you'd better go."

Blackie gazed at her long and hard. For the briefest moment she thought she detected a look of self-loathing in his eyes. Then he stalked out of the trailer, slamming the door behind him.

The rest of the night passed in a sort of blur. Quickly, so that she wouldn't have time to dwell on the events of the past hour, Jenny changed into a skirt and blouse, and hurried over to Ann's trailer to meet Brad. She needed the company of close friends to blot out the memory of those moments in Blackie's arms. Those moments of anger and pain, his, as well as hers.

But later, after returning to her own trailer, she realized nothing would ever erase certain scenes from her mind. Blackie despised her for not believing in him and throwing the ring in his face. In his pain, he'd wanted to see her suffer.

After what had happened, Jenny knew she'd never get to sleep that night. She couldn't bear to stay in the trailer when everything reminded her of Blackie.

On impulse, she locked her door and walked down the track and along the highway to the restaurant, purposely avoiding a glance in the direction of Blackie's trailer. Her shift began in less than five hours. Now was a perfect time to start inventory of the supply room, a project every manager disliked. But until she went on duty, the job would keep her busy and out of sight.

Maybe doing something tedious would help her regain control. She had to be reasonably alert to conduct the interview with the person applying for the dishwasher position later that morning. Blackie couldn't wait to be replaced, but whenever she envisioned him leaving O'Brien's for good, she experienced a shattering sense of loss.

"So THERE you are!" Jenny nerves were so frayed Sharlene's voice caused her to drop her clipboard. "The boss has been looking for you."

Jenny blinked. "What time it it? I forgot my watch."

"Quarter after seven."

"I'll be right there. Thanks, Sharlene." She felt the room sway as she bent over to pick up the clipboard. Trying not to draw attention to herself, she grabbed the nearest shelf for support.

"Sure. I told him you had to be around here somewhere. You're the only person I know who's never late for work. See you."

Jenny was so relieved to be left alone again she barely registered the compliment. She needed another minute to pull herself together and thanked providence Blackie was already at his post so she wouldn't risk bumping into him on her way to the office.

When she appeared in Tom's doorway seconds later, he shook his head. "You look terrible, kiddo. Come and sit down."

Jenny sank into the chair opposite his desk, dizzy from lack of sleep and overwhelmed by despair.

He leaned against the edge of the desk with his arms folded. "I don't know who's in worse shape. You or Blackie."

Jenny gasped at the mention of his name and stared searchingly at Tom. "I take it you've seen him this morning."

Tom gave her a weary nod. "At the crack of dawn he came to my trailer looking like a survivor of World War III and told me he was leaving. His gear was all packed on his motorcycle."

"He's *gone?*" Jenny let out a low moan.

"I'm afraid so. He wanted me to know the engagement was off. Permanently. He also said a good journalist never dealt in slander." Tom lifted one eyebrow. "He added a rider. He said that if and when he found a woman to spend the rest of his life with, he'd make certain she wasn't chained to a demented old guard dog like yours truly."

"Oh, Tom!" Jenny cried out in anguish, then hid her face in her hands. She started to sob and felt Tom's arms go around her heaving shoulders.

"As I see it, he forgot to add 'meddling idiot.' That's what I am, Jenny O'Brien."

She shook her head. "It's not your fault, Tom. I should have been honest with Blackie right from the beginning. Then none of this would've happened."

He sighed heavily. "Your instincts were right, Jenny. You knew Blackie loved you for yourself."

"Not anymore." Her voice shook.

"Right now that man doesn't know which end is up. He's run off to lick his wounds."

"He's gone," Jenny stated flatly. "And he'll never come back. Not after last night." The words trembled on her lips. "He wouldn't listen to any explanations. I've lost him, Tom." She gulped down a sob.

He hugged her hard. "Nobody knows what the future holds. But right now here's what you're going to do, and I'm the boss so you'll have to mind me. I want you to go back to your trailer and get some sleep. Today Marva's washing dishes and I'm planning to interview the new applicant. You're not to report until tomorrow morning. That's an order."

Slowly Jenny got to her feet. "You must be sick to death of me and my problems. I'm noted for causing trouble, and I'd hate to think you kept me on out of obligation to Dad."

For the second time since she'd known Tom, he looked angry. "I don't want to hear any more of that kind of talk. I've trained dozens of people for manager positions, and I've never been more impressed with anyone's performance than yours. Ask anyone here and they'll tell you the same thing. You're in too much pain to know what you're saying. Go back to the trailer and lie down, Jenny. Later I'll send over Marva to check on you."

"Thank you, Tom." She started for the door, then turned. "There's one more thing. I want everyone to know who I really am. After what's happened, I'm afraid to risk alienating anyone else. Do you have a suggestion as to how I should go about it?''

He nodded. ''Why don't you compose a letter we can photocopy and stick in everyone's mailbox. It doesn't have to be long and drawn out. Tell them the simple truth, straight from the heart. People are basically kind and they'll accept your explanation.''

Except Blackie. ''I'll do it.''

''It can wait a day, Jenny. You and Blackie have been through something traumatic and it shows.''

She took a deep breath. ''I appreciate what you're saying, but in spite of what's happened, I'll feel better when everyone knows the truth.''

''You have a lot of courage, Jennifer O'Brien. Your father would be proud of you.''

Jenny gave Tom a tremulous smile, then again turned to leave.

''Wait a minute, Jenny. I forgot to give you this.'' He opened the center desk drawer and pulled out a book. ''Blackie asked me to return this. He said it was yours.''

She took the mystery novel from him and hurried out of his office, feeling distinctly ill. The dining room was bustling with activity, and she had to weave her way around tourists and truckers to exit the restaurant.

As she neared their trailers, she saw that all traces of Blackie were gone. Without the motorcycle, his place looked deserted. Unable to bear it, Jenny dashed inside her own trailer. Once she'd locked the door, she braced herself against it, hardly capable of putting one foot in front of the other. The emptiness was so profound she sank down on the couch in a daze. For a while, she did nothing but stare into space.

Was Blackie still in California? Had he flown to New York? Vermont? She'd never know, never see him again. Her only communication would be the words he'd continue to write out for millions of people, instead of a personal message of love meant for her alone.

Their brief love affair had become a horror story and he wanted no part of it. She'd been labeled all her life, but nothing had hurt more than Blackie's words when he'd called her Mrs. Hyde.

A strange lethargy crept over her and she stretched full-length on the couch. Before she knew it, she was asleep.

Around two, she woke up and staggered into the tiny kitchen for a drink and perhaps some cheese or fruit. There were a couple of Cokes and root beers in the refrigerator, another painful reminder of Blackie. Was this the way it would be from now on? For the rest of her life? She shuddered at the thought and closed the refrigerator door, still empty-handed. Food was the last thing she could face right now.

It felt so strange to be alone. Blackie had filled every waking moment, had formed the texture of her dreams. Now that he was gone, she didn't have the faintest idea how she was going to function. Not even her father's death had affected her like this.

As if it had a will of its own, her hand drifted to the book lying on the table. A tight band around her chest constricted her breathing when she looked at the cover of *The Memphremagog Massacre*. She could still remember the first day when he'd commandeered it, the way those intelligent eyes had challenged hers from that impossibly handsome face.

Images of Blackie darted through her mind. Images of Blackie astride his motorcycle with his hair slightly windblown. Blackie gazing into the desert night. Once or twice, when he wasn't aware of her presence, she'd been surprised by a darkly remote quality on his face, as if he were miles away, deep in thought. But mostly she recalled his brilliant blue eyes, which ignited with desire every time he looked at her. And his sensual mouth, which more often than not curved into a wicked little smile before he kissed her.

Like the changing patterns in a kaleidoscope, brief flashes of the Blackie she adored came back to haunt her. That piratical grin when he was about to pull her under the water, the myriad shades of his blue eyes illuminated by the sunset, the delicious rasp of his jaw against her cheek at one in the morning. The taste of his mouth when it hungrily covered hers at unexpected moments.

Hot salty tears dropped one after the other. Suddenly she shoved the book away from her and threw herself on the bed, praying for oblivion.

JENNY WOULD NEVER have survived the next month if she hadn't worked almost around the clock and spent every spare moment with Sharlene helping Ann get ready for her wedding. She succeeded in staying so busy she fell into bed every night too exhausted to cry herself to sleep the way she'd done in the beginning.

True to Tom's prediction, the employees took the news of Jenny's real identity in their stride. If anything, her honesty increased the feeling of camaraderie.

However, her broken engagement and Blackie's unexpected departure were another matter altogether. By now, his identity, too, had been revealed. His series on truckers and waitresses was appearing weekly, and Tom had extra copies of one of the major L.A. papers, which carried Corbin Blackwell's column, delivered to the restaurant. He'd called a staff meeting to tell everyone about Blackie—carefully avoiding any mention of Jenny. So the secret was out: the Blackie they all loved was in reality the famous Corbin Blackwell. Everyone studied the columns avidly, searching for references to O'Brien's in the Mojave, hoping to see their own names in print. They weren't disappointed. And somehow, that made Blackie's absence a little less mournful.

But not for Jenny. She had the awkward task of explaining to her co-workers that her relationship with Blackie hadn't worked out because he was a loner at heart. He needed his freedom to pursue stories all over the world, she told them. Once again she found herself acting a part, pretending to be glad, for Blackie's sake, that he'd gone. Pretending he hadn't taken her heart with him. But when she was alone, she read his columns over and over again, often discussing them with Sharlene, the only person she hadn't managed to fool.

Now that Ann had married and moved to San Diego with Brad, Sharlene was the only one of her friends who kept pressing for more details about Blackie. She wasn't convinced Jenny had told her the whole story.

But Jenny wasn't ready to talk about it. She doubted she ever would be.

One of the few things that helped Jenny push Blackie to the back of her mind were her visits to town with Sharlene to see Stan. Jenny recognized how hard her friend had to work to keep Stan in a good facility and wished she could find a way to relieve Sharlene of some of her burden.

One evening after work, she found Sharlene waiting for her as she walked up the track to her trailer. "There you are. Come and have a drink with me. What with those busloads of tourists coming in at all hours today, I've barely had a chance to talk to you."

Jenny followed her inside. "Is Stan worse?" she asked immediately. Sharlene's husband was failing quite rapidly, and Jenny wanted to be there for her, if only as a shoulder to cry on.

After pouring them each a root beer, Sharlene took a seat on the couch next to Jenny. "It's no secret that Stan's condition is deteriorating all the time. But right now I have Mr. Dangerous on the brain. I got a long letter from him yesterday."

At that admission, Jenny almost lost her grip on the glass. She lifted her head and stared at the other woman in pained surprise. But Sharlene kept on talking, seemingly unaware of Jenny's chaotic emotions.

"You could've knocked me over dead when I found out he's not only Corbin Blackwell, but L. E. Boyd, the famous mystery writer. I swear I don't know how you or Blackie kept a straight face. I guess he told you the mystery he was working on here at O'Brien's was dedicated to me!" She beamed. "I hope it didn't hurt your feelings, Jenny, considering you're the one he fell in love with.''

L. E. Boyd. Jenny numbly repeated the name to herself, hearing little of Sharlene's happy chatter. Half-dazed, she got to her feet. "L. E. Boyd." She finally spoke the name out loud. *"Blackie is L. E. Boyd?"*

Sharlene's eyes grew huge. "You mean you didn't know?"

Jenny shook her head in absolute shock. "I had no idea."

"Well, if that doesn't beat all!" Sharlene muttered softly. "Everything's right here in the letter if you want to read it, Jenny. How he has to keep his writer's name a secret so he can get inside people's minds without them knowing anything about it. How sorry he is if he hurt anyone's feelings, how much he loved being with all of us, the parties and so on."

She could hear Sharlene talking but Jenny's mind had started going over everything from the very beginning. Like the unraveling of a plot, the odd remark, certain fragments of conversation, started falling into place faster than she could assimilate them, and she realized it was true. He'd come to the desert for a story, but it was a story that had nothing to do with Jenny O'Brien. And he'd accused *her* of lying!

Out of breath, she whirled around to face Sharlene. "Aren't you the least bit upset Blackie was using you as copy for his story?"

"Upset?" Her brows shot up. "I've never been so flattered in my life. Out of all the waitresses in the United States, he picked *me* for his research. Why, if he'd told me his real name when he first got here, I'd have been so ga-ga over him my brain would have turned to mush. You'd have had a wipe me off the floor like spilled chicken-giblet gravy.''

The picture she presented made Jenny laugh in spite of the shocking news, but then her smile faded. ''He said people step out of character when they know his real name.''

''Well, I'm sure I would have. Corbin Blackwell— that's incredible enough, but L. E. Boyd? I'm a mystery fan, and he's my all-time favorite author.'' She paused for a moment. ''You know, when I asked him why he wanted to talk shop with me instead of you, he told me he had other plans for you that had nothing to do with writing. He said that for once in his life he was going to go slow and easy, and didn't want anyone rocking the boat until he was ready.'' Her expressive pale eyebrows rose again.

''I got his drift in a big hurry. Of course, after that he went after you like a runaway train! The poor man was so crazy about you I didn't know if he'd last till you said your 'I do's.' ''

Her words brought fresh pain, though Jenny tried to steel herself against it. ''Sharlene, how do you know he didn't say things about you in the book that you wouldn't want made public?''

Sharlene stared at Jenny as if she'd come from another planet. ''Wow. That must have been some fight you had with Blackie. Otherwise you'd know he'd never deliberately hurt anybody. In fact, along with his letter, he sent what are called the galleys of his book and asked me to read them carefully, in case there was anything I didn't think was accurate. He won't let it get printed without my approval.''

Her words had a chastening effect on Jenny. "Have you had a chance to read it yet?"

"I stayed up all night to finish it."

"And *do* you approve?"

Sharlene's face sobered. "Do you want to know the truth?"

"Yes."

"When Stan had to go into the nursing home, I started reading to get my mind off things. I think I must have read everything out there, especially mysteries, like I said. Including Blackie's. But I'll tell you something. This book takes the cake. That man's a genius with a capital *G!*"

As Jenny listened with rapt attention, Sharlene got up from the couch and started pacing. "It's the story of a serial killer and it's the most terrifying thing I ever read. I'm not sure it ought to go into print." She raised brows for emphasis. "It might give some psychotic killer ideas. I'm trying to figure out how anyone as terrific as Mr. Dangerous could think up something so horrifying."

A chill ran through Jenny's body. "Did he portray you . . . or any of us in a bad light?"

Sharlene frowned. "What are you so worried about? None of us is in the book. What he did was get ideas from watching us work. It's a masterpiece. A bloodcurdling, spellbinding masterpiece. The kind of thing that'll be made into a movie for sure."

"You're joking!"

"You'll have to read it, then you'll know what I'm talking about. I'm not sure how he did it, but he got inside the mind of this truck driver who travels across the country and goes berserk killing waitresses. And you just keep reading and holding your breath because of the way the man thinks and plans his next move. I tell you, I don't know if I'm ever going to have a good night's sleep again.''

Her remark triggered something in Jenny's memory. ''He told me he interviewed some killers. In fact, when he applied for the job here, he said he'd driven a semi and talked with truckers, just to get the feel for their work.''

Sharlene nodded. ''That's why his books sell like hotcakes. They're dynamite.''

''I'd like to read it.''

''Sure. But I still can't figure out why he kept everything a secret from you. After all, the man asked you to marry him!''

Jenny nodded. ''But what's worse, he proposed to me before he knew I was Jenny O'Brien, only I thought he knew the truth and was just after my money and—''

''Wait a minute,'' Sharlene interrupted. ''Start from the beginning. I swear you've got me confused.''

Jenny hadn't thought she could talk to anyone about Blackie, but Sharlene had become a dear friend and was closer to Blackie than anyone she knew. Jenny suddenly found herself pouring out her heart.

When she'd finished, Sharlene sat there and shook her head. ''I never heard of such a mess. In fact I can't understand how two intelligent, beautiful people who are crazy about each other could have bungled things so badly. Why aren't you doing something about it?''

Jenny folded her arms. ''Because Blackie never wants to see me again. I accused him of wanting to marry me for my money when he's a millionaire in his own right."

"But you didn't know that at the time. Under the circumstances, I can see why Tom was worried enough to want to protect you. There are a lot of creeps out there who'd do anything to get their hands on twenty million dollars. But in all fairness to Blackie, there'd be a lot of women who'd like to spend *his* money, too! He probably didn't want you to know he was L. E. Boyd because he wanted to be loved for himself. If anyone could understand that, *you* could."

Jenny's heart pounded heavily in her chest as she recalled those exact words from Blackie on their drive home the night of the horror film. But she'd thrown them back in his face, not able to believe he was sincere.

A low moan escaped her throat. "None of it matters anymore. He hasn't tried to get in touch with me. The fact that he wrote you and told you the truth means it's really over between us. He knew word would get around. He also knew how it would make me feel to hear it from someone else."

"I don't know." Sharlene eyed her speculatively. "Maybe he decided telling me the truth was the only way to get through to you. After accusing *you* of being dishonest, he probably worried you'd tear up his letter or hang up on him if he called, and rightly so. After all, he left O'Brien's without giving you a chance to explain."

"I don't know what to think." Jenny turned to leave, her thoughts and emotions in turmoil. Was Blackie attempting to reach out to her through Sharlene?

"Here. Don't forget this." Sharlene handed her the galleys of Blackie's manuscript. The address of his New York publisher was on the outside of the padded envelope. Was Sharlene right? *Was* Blackie hoping she'd try to get in touch with him at that address? She closed her eyes tightly, afraid to believe it might be true.

"Thanks," she murmured. Hugging the package to her chest, she left Sharlene's and hurried to her own trailer. But instead of curling up on the couch to read Blackie's story, she pulled out pen and paper and began to write a letter.

CHAPTER TEN

WHEN THREE WEEKS had gone by and there'd been no word from Blackie, Jenny didn't know if he'd received her letter and ignored it, or if it was lying somewhere in a mail room, unread and forgotten.

To add to her turmoil, Blackie's column didn't appear in the paper anymore, which filled her with alarm. Once the series on truckers and waitresses came to an end, that was it. No explanations, no columns. *What had happened to him?*

Unable to bear the suspense any longer, she phoned the New York publisher. When she asked if Blackie had received her letter, she was told all mail meant for their authors was automatically forwarded to them, but that their addresses were kept confidential.

She hung up the phone in despair. The first step toward a reconciliation with Blackie had been futile, and she didn't even have his weekly column to keep him close to her anymore. If he'd chosen to ignore her entreaties, then she had to face the fact that she'd lost him forever.

The thought was so intolerable she drove to Santa Barbara on her next two-day break and tried to get away from memories of Blackie by going through her father's things. There were decisions to make about what to keep and what to discard. The task occupied all her waking hours, but didn't prevent her from missing Blackie with a desperation that caused physical pain.

Although she enjoyed the unobtrusive company of the Riveras, the house no longer felt like home now that her father was gone. Jenny discovered she was homesick for O'Brien's and the friends she'd made there. She missed her work. Most of all, she was haunted by Blackie's memory and wondered how she'd survive the rest of her life without him. She couldn't imagine ever falling in love again.

Jenny knew she should have phoned Vi and made arrangements to have lunch with her. But she was afraid of breaking down in front of the older woman, and that would accomplish nothing except to intensify her heartache. Jenny's only recourse was to return to the desert and immerse herself in work.

She drove into the trailer court at eleven-thirty in the evening and experienced a sense of homecoming when several of her friends gathered round wanting to know about her trip. They followed her inside the trailer and stayed long enough to have a drink and share a few laughs about their workday before turning in.

When they'd gone she showered and got ready for bed, slipping into a cool filmy nightgown. Because the drive from Santa Barbara usually made her tired, she thought she'd fall asleep as soon as she slid beneath the covers. But to her surprise she was still awake a half hour later.

Her glance darted automatically to the galleys of Blackie's manuscript sitting on her bedside table. Until now she hadn't been able to bring herself to read them, but tonight she was desperate to have some contact, any contact, with him. And she couldn't seem to sleep, anyway.. . .

From the first electrifying sentence the story was so riveting she became totally absorbed in it. She lost all awareness of the passage of time.

Sharlene hadn't exaggerated. The story was horrifying, but magnificently written. Jenny couldn't put it down. When she heard someone knock softly on her door, it seemed to be part of the very fabric of the book and she felt her blood chill.

The knocking persisted. She sat rigidly up in bed, immobilized. It was two o'clock in the morning. Her visitor couldn't be Tom or one of the employees. People from O'Brien's always called out and identified themselves on the spot. That was the unwritten law of the trailer court.

She held her breath and pretended to be asleep. After a few seconds she heard footsteps. Someone was walking around her trailer. On a fresh surge of adrenaline, she slid out of bed and tiptoed to the kitchen. Quietly she removed a pair of scissors from the drawer.

Whoever was out there could see the light and believed she was home. Maybe this person had seen her enter earlier and knew the trailers on either side of her had been empty for some time. No one would hear her if she screamed.

The knocking began again. "Jenny?" She heard her name called in a low unidentifiable voice. And then she saw the knob turn. If anyone wanted to get in, it wouldn't take much force to break down the door. Praying for courage, Jenny tiptoed over to it. "Who's there?"

"Mr. Hyde."

Blackie. She mouthed his name in utter disbelief. So many emotions flooded her almost simultaneously she couldn't speak.

"Jenny?" She could hear the concern in his deep rich voice. "I didn't mean to frighten you. I wasn't sure if you were there. I thought if I said Mr. Hyde you'd know beyond any doubt who was outside." There was a hesitant pause, then he went on, "I should have phoned from Los Angeles to tell you I was on my way, but I was afraid you'd refuse to talk to me. I can imagine how much you must despise me for lying to you. You have every right to tell me to go to blazes after the way I treated you."

Jenny ran a trembling hand through her hair, wondering if this was part of a dream. He obviously hadn't received her letter, so what did his being here now mean?

"You've got to forgive me, Jenny," he blurted in an anguished voice. "For the love of heaven, open the door. I've flown halfway around the world to see you."

Suddenly galvanized into action, she fumbled with the lock and opened the door. The scissors were still in her hand.

The color drained out of his face. "Dear Lord," he said in a haunted whisper, not moving any closer. "What have I done to you?"

It took Jenny a second to realize he was remembering the night he'd taken out his pain and frustration on her. He actually believed she'd armed herself against him.

"It's more a case of what your book has done to me," she hastened to assure him in an unsteady voice. "I've been reading the galleys you sent Sharlene. You're such a superb writer I was *living* the story, and when I heard your knock on the door my first instinct was to defend myself."

His chest heaved. "You of all people shouldn't be reading a book like that in the middle of the night, not when you're this isolated."

His searching gaze took in the pallor of her face, her tangled mane of hair, then traveled lower. A wave of heat swept over her body. In the joy of seeing him again, she'd forgotten she was still in her nightgown, and now she moved behind the partially closed door feeling unaccountably shy.

She took in the flesh-and-blood reality of the man she loved, and swallowed hard. Wearing a dazzling white shirt beneath a pearl-gray silk suit and tie, he was the image of sophistication. He looked every bit the famous writer and journalist.

Jenny feasted her eyes on him, trying to reconcile this grave, impossibly handsome stranger with the laughing, teasing Blackie who'd captured her heart. "W-why are you here?" she stammered at last, afraid to assume anything where he was concerned.

"You don't know?" He sounded like a man who'd had about all he could take. In an abrupt move he reached for her, but as he did the scissors fell from her hand.

She gasped slightly in surprise as one of the scissor points grazed the side of her foot.

Blackie cursed. Ashen-faced, he slammed the trailer door shut, then picked her up in his arms and carried her the short distance to the couch.

"Let me look." He set her down and lifted her foot for his inspection. "It's not deep." As he spoke, his thumb made lazy circles against her instep, sending waves of delight through her body. "Do you have any gauze? Any tape?" he asked thickly. She could see a nerve hammering along his lightly shadowed jaw.

"Yes," she murmured, more in a daze from the feel of his hands against her bare skin than anything else. "In the bathroom medicine cabinet."

With seeming reluctance he allowed her foot to slide out of his grasp before he turned away to get the bandages. The brief respite helped Jenny deal with the realization that it was Blackie rummaging around her bathroom like a nervous expectant father whose wife had gone into labor. The bittersweet thought twisted her emotions.

In a moment he was back and knelt down to bandage her foot. Delicious tremors vibrated through her body at his touch. Suddenly his dark head lifted and his startling blue eyes locked with hers. She suspected he wasn't aware his hands were caressing her leg, but it was all she could think about.

It had been five weeks since she'd known the fire of his kiss. Blackie's touch would always have the power to excite her. Afraid he could sense the hunger, she eased her leg from his grasp and got to her feet, hugging her arms to her chest.

"You left before I could return your ring." She seized on the first thing that came to her mind. "I would've sent it to your publisher in New York, but I hesitated because I didn't know who'd be signing for it. I also didn't know if I should send it in care of Corbin Blackwell or L. E. Boyd. Especially after you didn't seem to get my letter.''

Blackie's mouth thinned, and he stood up, a bleak look entering his eyes. "You sent me a letter?" His hands slid into the pockets of his suit jacket, as if he was having difficulty controlling them.

Jenny nodded mutely.

"I didn't know." He groaned. "How can I expect you to forgive me for not telling you the whole truth about myself when I wouldn't listen to you?"

Jenny looked up at him searchingly. "Why didn't you tell me? Couldn't you have trusted me?"

His chest heaved. "I'm no different from you, Jenny. I came to the Mojave on business and fell madly in love with a woman who knew nothing about my career as a novelist, who took me exactly as she found me in spite of her objections to my job, and didn't make me out to be some kind of god because my name was L. E. Boyd. Because I'm human, Jenny, with all the same needs and fears as the next person."

Jenny knew exactly what he was talking about and listened with her heart in her throat.

"Try to understand how I felt, Jenny. I wanted to prove to you that a stable home life meant as much to me as it did to you. But if I'd told you in the beginning that I was a novelist on top of everything else, I was afraid it would scare you off. We'd spent a lot of time together. I knew what your father's preoccupation with his work had done to you. Somehow I had to make you see that I wasn't a bit like him. On the contrary, I think I've always been a homebody at heart, but I needed a body at home with me. Your body, Jenny. Do you understand what I'm telling you?''

His explanation filled her with happiness. She couldn't talk, couldn't answer, while she struggled to absorb the words that poured from his soul.

"Jenny, have I done so much damage that you can't wait to be rid of me, can't bear to let me near you?'' He searched her face. "Maybe it's too much to ask. After the things I said to you the last time we were together in this trailer, I don't have the right to ask anything of you. I'm sorry if I've intruded. I swear I'll go away and never bother you again if that's what you want."

She shivered as she felt his gaze move intimately over her body, clad only in the brief nightgown. "I— I need my robe," she murmured shakily, and dashed into the bathroom in search of it. When she returned to the living room, she noticed Blackie had shed his suit coat and tie and had helped himself to a Coke. It was almost like old times and her heart began to hammer.

He looked wonderful standing in her living room, filling her trailer with his strong vital presence. Breathless, she sank onto the couch again. His eyes fastened on hers for a long speechless moment.

"Jenny," he said quietly, "let me tell you how it was after Helen died. As you know, I ran in all directions to try to deal with the pain. For more than two years I traveled all over the globe, doing various jobs to keep me going. When the pain finally stopped and I'd saved enough money, I decided I'd better get on with my education, so I went to university."

He leaned back against the counter. "I got a degree in economics, something my father had encouraged me to do because he said I'd need that kind of foundation if I wanted to be successful in a career. I'd always valued his opinion. However, working on Wall Street after graduation held no particular appeal for me and I found myself wanting to get back into reporting.

"I come from a long line of newspaper people, and that, combined with my travels, led me to pursue a career as a journalist. So I hired on with a newspaper and over the next ten years, I worked my way up the ladder. Some of the stories I covered began to fascinate me and I found myself writing novels on the side. To my complete surprise, the very first one became a best-seller and eventually I began enjoying real financial success.

"Not only was I able to write full-time, I could move around and avoid putting down roots. I was afraid that if I did, if I made a commitment to a woman, a home, my happiness might be snatched away a second time." He paused and stared at her with penetrating eyes. "I won't lie to you and pretend there haven't been other women. They provided a distraction from time to time but made no lasting impact on my life because I never intended to fall in love again or marry.

"My nomadic existence suited me perfectly until I found myself entangled with an exquisite red-haired witch who was all alone in the world, making a valiant effort to succeed without anyone's help. Everyone loved you and wanted to be your friend.

"But I wanted to be a great deal more than that. I discovered I wanted to be your lover, your husband. I wanted the right to protect you and take care of you. I realized I wanted to risk loving again. And to my joy, you appeared to return my love. Not because I was Corbin Blackwell, or L. E. Boyd, but because you loved me, Blackie." Her eyes closed at the fervency of his tone.

"The night we went out to look at the stars, I planned to tell you everything and hoped to surprise you with the news that I was buying the newspaper and settling down to a nine-to-five job. For the first time in years, I was glad I had enough money to be able to change careers—because it was what you wanted.

"But when you accused me of marrying you for your money and I found out you were Jennifer O'Brien, my world turned upside down. Not because of your reputation or your past, but because I knew you didn't *need* me for anything. The pain made me a little insane, and for a time I had to get away from you and O'Brien's and the desert. I had to go where I could try to make sense of my nightmare. What could I offer a woman who literally had everything?"

Jenny jumped to her feet, unable to stay seated with so many emotions bursting inside her. "How can you say that when you yourself lectured me that money doesn't necessarily bring security? Let me tell you what my life was like living with one parent who worked day and night to amass a fortune." While she spoke, she had to continually wipe the tears from her eyes.

"My world revolved around living in a fabulous mansion waiting for Daddy to come home and be with me. I adored my father and would've willingly traded my wealthy, pampered existence for a normal home life in a two-bedroom bungalow if it meant he'd spend some time with me. When it became clear I was waiting in vain, I started hanging around with other wealthy kids who were just as lonely and empty as I was. It was an aimless, unhappy existence, but it was all I had.

"And then, when men started to notice me as a woman, I was pursued constantly, but I never knew if it was for me or my money. Even very wealthy men were only interested because I had as much or more—that was what made me acceptable. Every time a man proposed, another layer of ice seemed to build up around my heart. I couldn't take anyone seriously because inside I was frozen. I had no real feelings.

"If a man tried to get close to me physically, I was repulsed and moved on to someone else, but most of the men I dated were insecure and accused me of being frigid. Out of wounded pride they made up stories about my loose morals. Sometimes my name appeared in the gossip columns and my father would try to get things hushed up. It was about the only time he paid any attention to me, but after one particular nasty article, he was really upset, and that's when I left for Europe." Her voice wavered.

"I thought any interest on his part was better than none, but the disappointment in his eyes haunted me and I partied harder than ever, trying to bury the pain. It was at this point that Vi wired my hotel with the news that Daddy had suffered a heart attack. But I was on the Varoz yacht, and by the time word reached me, he was gone," she whispered, still feeling the emptiness of that moment.

"I came close to falling apart when I heard what had happened. Not only because of the loss, but because I'd never found the courage to talk to Daddy about Mother. We never discussed the pain he suffered over losing her, yet I knew he'd been deeply affected by her death. I was afraid to mention her name for fear he'd close up even more. Vi had to be the one to make me understand.

"She'd been a silent bystander over ten years and understood my father as no one else could have because she loved him, too. After the funeral, I was in a daze. Daddy had left me the controlling interest in the company, but no one liked me or trusted me, and the company wanted me out of its hair. I was literally bribed by some of board members to sell out." She lifted tearful eyes to Blackie.

"I didn't know what to do, where to turn. If it hadn't been for Vi's faith in me, I'm not sure what would have happened. She told me to hold on to the company and challenged me to learn the business. It was her suggestion that I train under Tom. She was convinced my father would never have left everything to me if he hadn't wanted me involved.

"Maybe it's because I wanted to believe her so much that I thought it over and decided to try. But I was terrified Tom would never hire me if he knew who I was, so with Vi's help and approval, I applied for the trainee-manager's position as Jenny Connelly. I intended to tell Tom the whole truth just as soon as I'd worked there a while and proved I wasn't as bad as my reputation made me out to be.

"Somehow I managed to pass Tom's interview and started training. Everything went better than I dared hope. Tom was wonderful to me and started treating me more like a daughter than an employee. When I was told to interview you for the job, I realized he trusted me completely."

"Do you mean to say I was your first interview?" Blackie demanded incredulously.

"Yes."

He shook his head. "For what it's worth, you handled yourself like a pro, Jenny. I ought to have been drawn and quartered for what I did to you."

She folded her arms tightly against her waist. "I have to admit you gave me some terrible moments, but I wanted to justify Tom's faith in me. Fortunately he acted pleased that I'd hired you, and everything seemed to go along all right, even when he found out I was really Jenny O'Brien."

At Blackie's inquiring look, she told him how that had come about. Then she said, "Tom had known my father well, and he told me how Mother's death had killed something in Daddy. His explanation helped me come to grips with a lot of feelings I hadn't resolved.

"He said I ought to keep my secret a while longer and praised me for trying to fill my father's shoes. He also worried that somehow *you'd* gotten wind of things and had applied for a job on the pretext of needing to do research, when in reality you were going to write an exposé on me and my father. He didn't want me to get hurt."

"I can understand that," Blackie said in an ago-
nized whisper, absently rubbing the back of his neck.
"Under the circumstances, I don't understand why
you're even talking to me. After the things I said and
did to you on the night of Sharlene's party, I can't
expect you to forgive me. Rest assured I'll never hurt
you again."

Before she could comprehend what was happening, Blackie gathered his tie and jacket and started for
the door. She couldn't let him go without telling him
the truth. "If you walk out now, it'll destroy me." Her
voice shook with raw need. "I'm in love with you,
Blackie. It's the painful kind of love that'll never go
away, no matter what's gone on in the past."

As if in slow motion, she saw him pause in midstride and wheel around. "What did you say?" His
eyes were ablaze with light. He drew closer.

"I love you so much it's agony, and I'm beginning
to understand why my father was never the same after Mother died. I'm afraid I'm just like him. I'm the
kind of woman who can love only one man, and that's
you, my darling."

She watched the tension flow out of him, and on his
face she saw the pure eager tremulous look of joy. The
years seemed to fall away, giving her a glimpse of a
younger carefree Blackie, one who now swept her up
in his powerful arms.

Jenny heard his low groan of satisfaction as she
tried to show him, tried to tell him, tried to let him
know in every way that she loved him.

"I love you, Jenny," he said after long minutes, fe-
verishly covering her face and neck with kisses. "To
be honest, I didn't know love could come to a person

the way it's been born in me—full-blown, total, cata-clysmic. I thought it grew bit by bit.

"When I carried you from the truck to your bed in the trailer that first day, loving you, desiring you, was instinctive. It was almost as if we'd loved each other in another life. It was the most marvelous sensation I've ever experienced. There was a *rightness* about holding you in my arms. And what made it so incred-ible was that you felt the same way."

Jenny buried her face in his neck. "I did. I felt ex-actly like you. I couldn't believe it. Even when Tom told me to be careful, you were already in my blood. When you left, I wanted to die."

He kissed a sensitive spot on her neck. "I prayed you'd get in touch with me."

"How could I have done that?" She bit his earlobe softly. "I had no idea where you were, and both your name and your mother's are unlisted. But after you sent Sharlene the manuscript, I wrote you a letter. When I didn't hear back, I phoned your publisher and they assured me my letter had been forwarded to you. I assumed you wanted nothing to do with me."

Blackie groaned and clasped her tighter. "It's probably with the rest of my mail in Newport. When I didn't hear from you, I wrote Sharlene, hoping she'd mention it so you'd try to reach me in New York."

"Sharlene thought that might be your plan." She smiled up at him.

"But I was too afraid you might not phone or write. I flew to Europe to research a story, but as you can well imagine, my heart wasn't in it. So I decided to pack it in.

"Since the only person who mattered to me was living right here in the Mojave, I took the first plane out of Paris and flew directly to Los Angeles. I couldn't get here fast enough. I need you, sweetheart," he murmured against her mouth.

Once more Jenny was caught up in a tide of sensual feeling. The reality of his physical presence was still too new and precious for her to do anything but savor it. She slid her arms around his neck, hugging him harder. "I need you that much more. Get ready to be loved by a woman who's not prepared to let you out of her sight for a single second."

Her words drew a shuddering response from Blackie, and he finally stopped kissing her long enough to cup her face in his hands. "What are we going to do? Do you want to stay here and work under Tom until you feel confident enough to head the company? I can write wherever you are. My only concern is that we be together. I've been alone too many years and I want to spend the rest of my days— and nights—with you."

"Is the newspaper still for sale?" she asked suddenly.

Her question seemed to surprise him. "Yes, but it's not important. All I care about is your happiness."

"I love you for saying that, but more and more I crave the idea of living in Newport near your family and helping you run a newspaper."

Blackie looked stunned. "But what about your father's company? I'm not going to be the one responsible for causing you to turn your back on it or your family home."

"I have no desire to be the head of O'Brien's, though I'd like to sit on the board and fly out to California to attend the monthly meetings—but you'll have to come with me. I've learned quite a bit already, and what I don't know I can discuss with Tom and my new husband, who can tutor me in economics when the occasion demands. As far as the house in Santa Barbara is concerned, I'm going to have it refurbished as a nursing home where people like Sharlene's husband can come for free medical care."

"Jenny—" his eyes shone like blue stars "—do you mean it?"

She tipped her head back to gaze up at him adoringly. "How can you possibly doubt it? I've been picturing our sons and daughters climbing trees in the backyard of that beautiful house you once said you had in mind. Is it for sale, too?"

"I already own it," he murmured, pressing a kiss of great tenderness on her mouth. "I bought it years ago. It's on Lake Memphremagog, just outside Newport, and not that far from the monastery I wrote about in my last book. It's a kind of talisman, if you like. Something to bring me back home if I ever found the right woman."

His declaration drew an ecstatic sigh from Jenny and once more they were kissing with a profound hunger. "Marry me as soon as possible?" he finally spoke on a ragged breath, touching his forehead to hers.

"My truck's full of gas. If you want we can drive to Las Vegas right now."

He shook his head and drew her into her arms. "No, Jenny. I have this vision of you floating down the aisle of the church in Newport with flowers in your beautiful hair, and my little nieces carrying your train. I want my family, our friends, the whole world to know how you honored me by becoming my wife.''

''Blackie.'' Her voice caught at the humility in his tone. ''I'm the one who's honored. I want to do everything for you, be everything to you.''

That heart-stopping smile broke out on his face. ''As I told you once before, you're stuck with me now, Mrs. Blackwell, morning, noon and night. Wherever we go, whatever we do, it'll be together.''

''Will you take me to the Sahara?''

He kissed her eyelids closed. ''I've already made the arrangements.''

She let out a little cry of joy, which he stifled with his mouth. ''What about...'' she began, but his lips made forays over her sensitized skin and she couldn't form another coherent thought.

''On a day far from now,'' he murmured, ''we'll talk about the rest of our lives. Right now, woman, I want to communicate with you on a much more elemental level.''

Jenny put her hand over his heart, and she knew it beat for her. She gazed up at him out of eyes brimming with love. ''Blackie's woman. How perfect,'' she whispered, tracing the slant of his dark brow with her finger.

Blackie's handsome face drew closer. ''Just how perfect you'll never know. Come here to me, sweetheart.''

This August, don't miss an exclusive
two-in-one collection of earlier love stories

MAN
WITH A PAST

TRUE COLORS

by one of today's hottest
romance authors,

Jayne Ann Krentz

Now, two of Jayne Ann Krentz's most loved books are
available together in this special edition that new and
longtime fans will want to add to their bookshelves.

Let Jayne Ann Krentz capture your hearts with the love
stories, MAN WITH A PAST and TRUE COLORS.

And in October, watch for the second two-in-one
collection by Barbara Delinsky!

Available wherever Harlequin books are sold.

HARLEQUIN

Romance

**This September, travel to England
with Harlequin Romance
FIRST CLASS title #3149,
ROSES HAVE THORNS
by Betty Neels**

It was Radolf Nauta's fault that Sarah lost her job at the hospital and was forced to look elsewhere for a living. So she wasn't particulary pleased to meet him again in a totally different environment. Not that he seemed disposed to be gracious to her: arrogant, opinionated and entirely too sure of himself, Radolf was just the sort of man Sarah disliked most. And yet, the more she saw of him, the more she found herself wondering what he really thought about her—which was stupid, because he was the last man on earth she could ever love....

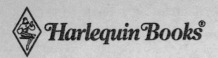
Harlequin Books®

GREAT NEWS...

HARLEQUIN UNVEILS NEW SHIPPING PLANS

For the convenience of customers, Harlequin has announced that Harlequin romances will now be available in stores at these convenient times each month*:

Harlequin Presents, American Romance, Historical, Intrigue:

> May titles: April 10
> June titles: May 8
> July titles: June 5
> August titles: July 10

Harlequin Romance, Superromance, Temptation, Regency Romance:

> May titles: April 24
> June titles: May 22
> July titles: June 19
> August titles: July 24

We hope this new schedule is convenient for you.

With only two trips each month to your local bookseller, you'll never miss any of your favorite authors!

*Please note: There may be slight variations in on-sale dates in your area due to differences in shipping and handling.

*Applicable to U.S. only.

HDATES-RR

Have You Ever Wondered If You Could Write A Harlequin Novel?

Here's great news—Harlequin is offering a series of cassette tapes to help you do just that. Written by Harlequin editors, these tapes give practical advice on how to make your characters—and your story—come alive. There's a tape for each contemporary romance series Harlequin publishes.

Mail order only

All sales final

Harlequin Superromance®

Available in Superromance this month
#462—STARLIT PROMISE

STARLIT PROMISE is a deeply moving story of a
woman coming to terms with her grief and gradually
opening her heart to life and love.

Author Petra Holland sets the scene beautifully, never
allowing her heroine to become mired in self-pity. It
is a story that will touch your heart and leave you
celebrating the strength of the human spirit.

**Available wherever Harlequin books
are sold.**